Death ot a College

by

Robert M. Dixon

To Dave Dennis
Best wishes for success
in The Algebra Project.
Robert M Dixon
12/23/2017

2017

Death of a College
by Robert M. Dixon
Copyright © 2013 by Robert M. Dixon

Contents

Preface

"Death of a College" is the story of the struggles of a mythical private, historically Black college to survive in the latter quarter of the twentieth century. Stonewood College, founded in 1871 in Savannah, Georgia, rose to prominence because of the success of its graduates. In 1978, following published news articles alleging mismanagement and theft of federal funds, the college entered an era of escalating problems, which challenged its purpose and its future. In particular, the enrollment spiraled downward, debt mounted, endowment funds were used, and the financial stability of the college was called into question by the regional accrediting agency, the Atlantic Association of Colleges and Schools (AACS). After the administration failed to meet the financial stability standard of AACS, the college was placed on probation in December 1983. This resulted in the board dismissing the president and conducting a national search to find a person who could lead the institution to stability and national prominence.

This is where the story begins with the selection of Dr. Jason E. Hammer as president and his endeavor to lead the college. Although informed by my experience in higher education, the story is fictional and any similarity to any persons living or deceased is coincidental. Some of the challenges faced by Stonewood are known and experienced by many colleges and universities. It is a fact that many of the historically Black colleges and universities (HBCU) during the last twenty-five years of the twentieth century and early in the twenty-first century found their futures bleak due to difficulties with regional accreditation. Examples are Knoxville College, Fisk University, Bishop College, Morris Brown College, Barber-Scotia College, and Saint Paul's College. Only Fisk continued to operate at the end of 2013 as a regionally accredited institution. Several of the public HBCU have had accreditation challenges; however, unlike many of the private institutions, they operate today as accredited universities.

Indeed, this fictional account of the saga of Stonewood College may at times intersect or approach authentic events and authentic human behavior. The play, in title only, is reminiscent of *Death of a Salesman* by Arthur Miller. Whereas Miller's tragic hero, Willie Loman, struggles to recapture an era, in *Death of a College*, the tragic hero, Stonewood College, struggles to possess a future that its stewards are not prepared to accept. As the story unfolds, the potential for success opens again and again only to be undermined by human frailty. Time challenges the existence of institutions that cannot adjust to changing circumstances - that cling to outmoded practices and paradigms. *Death of a College* is an American story, rich with all the subtexts that permeate many of our institutions and, ultimately, limit their possibilities. Tragically, Stonewood's demise is charted by the confluence of conspiring forces that for a brief period align in such a way that its survival is not an option. Its journey should remind us of the fragility of our institutions and of how easily their futures, however greatly needed, can be compromised by emotion that displaces intellect and by moral and ethical lapses.

Robert M. Dixon
Atlanta, Georgia

CHARACTERS

Dr. Jason E Hammer

Attorney Samuel E Eagles

Mrs. Marva Rayson

Dean Waverly Bennings

Dr. Stan D. Zillaman

Dr. Louis J Tullson

Mr. Jackson R Stanmore

Reverend Belvin Winter

Mrs. Alexa Bastrap

Dr. Alma Y Lemon

Reverend Justin Raymondale

Dr. Martin Melvins

Dr. Anne Blakemon

Mr. Nathan C Bessel

Ms. Jane LaPortier

Mrs. Lynne Alice Wynn

Dr. Roland Saint-Amand

Mr. Marcus Turnipseed

Ms. Tameka Kellogan

Ms. Skyla Renee Dickenson

Mr. Devarious Watersmith

Ms. Kyla Anne Author

Mr. Walter Shreve

Mrs. Kimberly Castleburg

Mr. David Kensmith (Voice only)

Trustee Avers

Trustee Bellmede

Reverend Albert Densley

Trustee Pauls

Trustee Velcome

AACS Committee Member

AACS Committee Chairman

Trustees Avers, Bellmede, Densley, Pauls and Velcome have non-speaking roles except for voice votes during board meetings.

The Place and Time

The boardroom in the Administration Building at Stonewood College, a private, historically Black college (HBC) located in Savannah, Georgia, the president's office, the kitchen of a trustee, the podium in the college chapel, a meeting room in a Miami hotel, and a sitting area in the lobby of the hotel. The events portrayed take place between 1984 and 1989.

ACT I

Probation and Problems Revealed

The music Pomp and Circumstance is heard in the background. It plays for several minutes. The sound intensity (volume) of the music is reduced. The curtain slowly rises with the lights on the boardroom. The president's office adjoins the boardroom. Through the windows at the far end of the boardroom one can see in the distance one of the college's thirty-two buildings against a blue and sunny sky. The boardroom, which is located stage right (as seen from the audience), has a twenty-foot long conference table arranged so that it extends from the windows toward the audience. Seven high back black leather chairs are located on each side of the table. A similar chair is located at the far end of the table, between the table and the windows. This is the chair used by the board chair and the college president. Two pictures of former presidents frame the windows. The right imaginary wall of the boardroom has no doors or windows and is used for entrances and exits by the character, who connects us with the past. The left imaginary wall contains a door to the president's office. The president's office, which is to the left of center stage, has an executive desk, a high back brown leather chair, a file cabinet, and a credenza on which sits an electronic typewriter. A window is located behind the credenza, which is behind the president's desk. The left imaginary wall in the president's office has a door leading to the office of the special assistant to the president. The special assistant's office is stage left and only a portion of the office can be seen by the audience. A portion of the desk and an electronic typewriter are visible to the audience. Thus, the special assistant may sometimes be seen by the audience. Board members and staff members and others enter and exit the boardroom via an imaginary door toward the front of the stage and on the imaginary left wall of the boardroom. The president always enters and exits the boardroom using the door between his office and the boardroom.

The music continues softly as the audience views the stage. A narrator's voice is heard.

Narrator. Stonewood College, a co-educational, historically Black, baccalaureate-degree granting institution, has fallen on hard times. Founded in 1871, Stonewood is highly regarded throughout the nation and, internationally, throughout the Caribbean and among West African countries. This once venerable institution has experienced a decline of 1,200 students over the last two years. The enrollment of full-time students declined from 5,000 to 3,800. The college has had difficulty in paying its bills and unsolicited contributions to it have decreased from between $50,000 to $100,000 per month to a few thousand dollars per month. The endowment, which five years ago exceeded thirty million dollars, today stands at almost eleven million dollars. Last January the college was placed on probation by the Atlantic Association of Colleges and Schools (AACS) for failure to demonstrate financial stability after having been on warning for two years. The last president was dismissed by the board of trustees the same week that the college was notified of its probationary status. The failure of the president to provide adequate leadership was cited in the board's letter of dismissal.

The board conducted a national search and selected Dr. Jason E. Hammer, who last worked as a special assistant to the President of Yale University. The trustees are meeting today, early in July, to welcome Dr. Hammer to the college, discuss the challenges faced, and to express their commitment to support him in leading the institution forward.
End of opening narration.

The trustees enter stage left and take seats in the boardroom. Dr. Hammer can be seen being shown into his office, which remains dark, by his special assistant, Mrs. Lynne Alice Wynn, where he quickly occupies himself reading reports found on his desk.

Narrator. Prior to meeting with President Hammer, the trustees are having a pre-meeting. Dr. Hammer is waiting in his office to be invited to join the trustees in the boardroom. The pre-meeting discussion is being led by Chairperson Samuel Edward Eagles, an alumnus and a successful lawyer. All twelve trustees are present.

The music ends.

Chair Eagles. We must impress on Dr. Hammer the urgency of our situation. We need, we must have immediate success. If we have any problems, raising money will be impossible. Our brand has been tarnished and many of our strongest supporters have adopted a wait and see attitude. Since January, we have lost three board members, who annually gave more than $200,000 to the college. The departure of these three white board members, all very successful in business, has damaged our reputation with the local business community. Their resignations have been interpreted by some people to mean that the local business community no longer supports Stonewood and to question our viability.

Trustee Martin Melvins interrupts the Chair. (Dr. Melvins is an assistant superintendent of schools in Saint Augustine, Florida.) Mr. Chairman, why did we hire this man? He never worked at an HBC. He was not in a leadership position and he has no real track record for raising money.

Chair Eagles. Dr. Melvins, I am surprised by your question at this stage. The man worked at Yale directly with the president. He had to be involved on a daily basis with all aspects of the running of the university. He has excellent contacts throughout …

11

Trustee Melvins. Those are Yale contacts – not Stonewood contacts. Selling Yale, if Hammer did that and I doubt it, is different than selling Stonewood. You know Mr. Chairman many special assistants don't report to the president. They may report to a vice president. I recall a president at the University of Maryland who had about a dozen special assistants. The joke was that he did not even know the names of these assistants. It's like saying you work in the Whitehouse. You might be in the Old Executive Office Building, or some other building and report to a deputy secretary of the agency related to your area of work. Would you claim to work with the President of the U. S.?

Chair Eagles. What is this I am hearing? You expressed none of this early in the selection process. In fact, Dr. Melvins you were supportive of Dr. Hammer. Yes, Dr. Blakemon.

Trustee Anne Blakemon. (Dr. Anne Blakemon is a local physician, whose late father attended Stonewood.) Yes, Dr. Mclvins: Why at this stage do you raise such questions? Whatever Dr. Hammer did or did not do at Yale is now immaterial. Dr. Hammer is our president and we must strive to make his tenure successful. We must be unified in our support; otherwise, we place Stonewood in grave jeopardy.

Trustee Melvins. We are already in grave jeopardy. Have been for the last ten years. I plan to do all that I can for the man. I just had some second thoughts.

Trustee Blakemon. Well good. Our problem is the Atlantic Association, which seems to be determined to close every HBC in the region.

Chair Eagles. That's true. At one point in time Atlantic refused to accredit HBC's. Then it created a special category for them until that proved embarrassing to the Association and the federal government. Now the game seems to be their elimination. The formula to achieve this is quite clear. Challenge anything using the guise of "institutional effectiveness." Once this is known to the public some enrollment decline is likely. Many of our institutions have small reserves, if any, so a small drop in enrollment can have a noticeable impact financially. Then financial stability can be used. If the examination by Atlantic extends for a period of time, the enrollment decline is likely to increase. If the decline grows, then a major struggle ensues. We are in such a struggle.

Trustee Melvins. Mr. Chair, just what is institutional effectiveness?

Chair Eagles. It is a term that has changed since it was first introduced. When Atlantic first started using it as a standard colleges did not have a clue about what was wanted. Daring not to insult the Atlantic Association, many schools responded by establishing an office of institutional effectiveness, with a director of institutional effectiveness. When it was first introduced, individuals in planning and institutional research were given the responsibility of responding to the standard. Today, it is used broadly. If a school does not have enough faculty members to offer a given program, or enough resources, or if it does not schedule enough sections of courses to meet the needs of students, then it is not an effective institution. It is a catchall. An institution might meet all the other standards, and fail to meet institutional effectiveness. You can be certain that there is arbitrariness in the accreditation process.

Trustee Blakemon. I did not think that the process was arbitrary.

Chair Eagles. I did not say the process is arbitrary. I said that there is arbitrariness in it, which enters through the selection of things to examine or not examine and then through the interpretation given. There was a school in Arkansas that had a library, which was largely unusable. The bottom floor was sealed off from the rest of the library. The bottom floor was covered with mold. The water table in the area where the library was constructed is so high that when it rains water enters the bottom floor. The library has beautiful glass on one side through which rain enters on all levels. The lighting is dramatically inadequate. Certain areas are so dimly lighted that they cannot be used. The temperature cannot be controlled, even in the special collections room.

Trustee Blakemon. I'll bet that school was found ineffective and placed on warning about its library.

Chair Eagles. No, the school had its accreditation reaffirmed. I was informed that the visiting committee chose not to visit the library. The process involves judgments, which we hope are not political although examples abound that it is quite political. Today ladies and gentlemen, our challenge is to show that Stonewood is financially stable.

Trustee Belvin Winter. (Reverend Winter is the pastor of a large Baptist church in Baton Rouge, Louisiana. He served as President of the Atlantic Baptist Conference for ten years.) Stonewood has meant so much to so many people here and abroad. We should have no trouble raising money and showing that the college is stable. With our support, Dr. Hammer will not have any problems.

Trustee Melvins. Reverend Winter, don't you realize that only about 5 percent of our alumni give to the college. We really don't have a history of raising money. In the past our president would raise two or three million dollars annually to balance the budget. In those days we were about a third of our current size. Twenty years ago Stonewood had a capital campaign and attempted to raise twenty-five million dollars. We reached eighteen million and the board declared the campaign to be a success.

Reverend Winter. I understand the challenges and the problems that we have faced in the past. I am here, as I believe you are, because I believe in this college and I believe that the current problems can and will be resolved. I am certain that we are equal to the task.

Chair Eagles. Trustees we have some long-range debt totaling twenty million dollars. We ended the fiscal year with a deficit of ten million dollars. We are projecting another drop in enrollment of two hundred students. Dr. Hammer will have to make some cuts and some major adjustments. Our situation is difficult and could easily spiral out of control. The threat posed by Atlantic has damaged our image. Even students ask their instructors if we are still accredited. Yes, Reverend Raymondale.

Trustee Justin Raymondale. (Reverend Raymondale is the senior pastor of a prominent church in Savannah.) I understand our situation and I tell you that Stonewood must come through this challenge. Now, there are some HBC's that are simply not going to make it and admittedly some should close. Few of them can match our accomplishments. Few of them can match our endowment, and few of them have the brand recognition that we enjoy. And, off the record Mr. Secretary, few of them have people of the caliber of the folks in this room working on their behalf. Actually, I am surprised about our current problems. We should not be in this position.

Trustee Marva Rayson. (Mrs. Rayson is a local businesswoman who owns cleaners, restaurants, and extensive rental property throughout Savannah.) Mr. Chair, although much of the conversation is useful, we are here to make certain that Dr. Hammer gets off to a good start. I think that we should bring Dr. Hammer in so that we can start.

Chair Eagles. Very well, without objection, Dr. Melvins please escort Dr. Hammer into the boardroom.

Dr. Melvins moves quickly to bring Dr. Hammer into the room. As Doctors Melvins and Hammer enter the room only Chair Eagles rises.

Chair Eagles. Welcome Dr. Hammer. Please be seated in the empty seat next to me. Before we proceed with the meeting I ask Reverend Justin Raymondale to lead us in prayer.

Reverend Raymondale. Dear God, we come humbly this afternoon seeking Your guidance and blessing. We ask that You lead us to make decisions and take actions that serve to maintain Stonewood College. We ask that You aid us to analyze, aid us to propose, and aid us to act in the best interest of those students whose hopes and dreams are bound to this institution. Just as You brought us through the difficult and trying times of reconstruction and segregation, we beseech You to be with us now in this dark hour and lead us to the light. Show us the way. We pray Your blessing on our deliberations. Amen.

Chair Eagles. Amen. Dr. Hammer met board members during his interview for the position of president several months ago. Therefore, we do not need to spend time with introductions. The purpose of this Call Meeting of the Board of Trustees of Stonewood College is to welcome President Hammer and to make certain that he fully understands the challenges that we face with respect to accreditation.

Dr. Hammer, we are grateful that you have accepted our offer to lead this historic institution. We commit ourselves to assist you in moving the college from probation to reaffirmation of accreditation by the Atlantic Association of Colleges and Schools. The journey will not be easy; however, we believe that you are the right person to lead this institution at this critical time. We know that changes will have to be made. We realize that some of what passes for tradition is simply archaic. You should know and remember that you have the backing and support of all constituents of the Stonewood community. In this we are unified, in this we are one.

Dr. Hammer. Thank you Chairman Eagles, I deliberated for a long time before accepting your offer. I was persuaded by Stonewood's outstanding history that every effort must be made to ensure its future. Many students need this college and many persons and other institutions need Stonewood to exist. I shall work hard to achieve the reaffirmation of accreditation by AACS. I shall present you with a plan to accomplish this by October 31. I realize that AACS requires a report in approximately fourteen months, which will determine our future. You must be prepared to take some different steps and make some difficult decisions. Our situation, though critical, is manageable. I am pleased that all members of our community are prepared to pull together in order to preserve Stonewood.

The plan that I shall present will take into account our strengths and address the problems cited by AACS. I shall conduct over the next two weeks a review of our major divisions, academic affairs, student affairs, financial affairs, and operations. I know that you have been candid with me about the challenges we face; however, I want to be certain that a review by a visiting committee from AACS will not uncover something about which no one knows. I may inquire of some of you about members of the Savannah business community, especially those who formerly were donors.

Together, we shall succeed in placing Stonewood College on a path toward a bright future.

Chair Eagles. Thank you President Hammer. I speak for the entire board when I say to you that we shall support you in advancing the college. As I listened to your remarks I was reassured that we are on a course that will lead to success.

Do we have questions for the president?

Trustee Melvins. Martin Melvins, sir. I serve as the Assistant Superintendent of Schools in Saint Augustine, Florida. Dr. Hammer, have you given any thought to making changes in the senior administrative team?

Dr. Hammer. I have given considerable thought to pros and cons of making changes at this time. Given the extraordinary circumstances, I believe that we will be better served by the existing set of administrators as we work our way to reaffirmation of accreditation. After that I expect to build a new team of senior administrators. Additionally, our current situation would inhibit many persons in the academy from applying.

Trustee Melvins. Exactly. So, why did you apply?

Trustee Blakemon. (Under her breath.) There he goes again.

Chair Eagles. Dr. Melvins, this is not an interview. Dr. Hammer has the job. He is our leader and

Dr. Hammer interrupts. I don't mind answering Dr. Melvins question. I believe that the HBC's would be stronger today if more African Americans in the academy would work at them. Although many of us did not attend an HBC, we benefited from the ethos that the existence of these institutions created in higher education in America. Their existence spoke to the importance of educational opportunity and provided motivation for majority institutions to seek African American students and scholars. Many majority institutions sought to distance themselves from a past that was antithetical to fairness, justice, and what we understand about human potential and development. Dr. Melvins, I believe that losing Stonewood threatens all HBC's and that it threatens equal educational opportunity in higher education. I believe in the mission of Stonewood College and I believe that we must do everything that we can to preserve the college. I chose to get in this fight because I believe in Stonewood and though I did not attend, I know that I owe Stonewood. You might say that I am here to pay a debt.

Trustee Raymondale rises to his feet and loudly proclaims: Amen, Amen, I knew that we had the right person for the job.

Trustee Melvins. Thank you Dr. Hammer.

Chair Eagles. Yes, Mrs. Rayson.

Trustee Rayson. Dr. Hammer, I am Marva Rayson. I am the owner of several businesses in Savannah. My father graduated from the college and supported it financially during his lifetime. I have continued his tradition. I just wondered if you knew that we have been abandoned by the business community. We had three influential and wealthy white businessmen resign from the board after AACS placed the college on warning. Also there is widespread talk in the community of corruption at the college. This talk has gone on since we were investigated about five years ago for mishandling a federal grant. Former President Foucault informed us in a phone conference that he had had a very ugly conversation with the Secretary of Health, Education and Welfare about the college's involvement in some federal programs. He told us that the secretary promised him that he would regret the conversation. The next day FBI agents were at the campus. They seized records involving federal programs. In a few weeks President Foucault, his special assistant, Juan Falcone, and the vice president for finance, Earl Teslane were indicted for fraud and theft. Teslane and the president were exonerated in court; however, Mr. Falcone was found guilty of theft and sentenced to five years in federal prison. Of course the press had a field day. Daily, we were on the front page, even when the articles contained no new content. Looking back, the president's conversation with the secretary marked the beginning of a difficult period in our history.

Dr. Hammer. I am aware of most of what you said. I did not know that the rapacious and aggressive nature of the investigation could be connected to personal difficulties between President Foucault and the Secretary of HEW. I am prepared to work to mend our relationships with the Department of Education, members of the business community, and the media.

Chair Eagles. Yes, Reverend Winter.

Reverend Winter. Dr. Hammer, I am Reverend Belvin Winter, a humble servant of God currently serving the good people at Field Street Baptist Church in Baton Rouge, Louisiana. Although I am quite a distance from Savannah, I want to invite you to visit and to speak at my church, Field Street Baptist. You are going to need students and I think you have to go after them broadly. I pledge my support to assist you in whatever way I can. In fact, we need money. I brought with me a small donation of $5,000.00 to help you along the way. This coming Sunday we are going to have a special offering, just for Stonewood.

Dr. Hammer. Thank you Reverend Winter. I am grateful for your support and I am encouraged by your generosity. You set a great example of the kind of support that we shall need in order to be successful. I look forward to visiting the famous Field Street Baptist Church. Just let me know when you would like for me to visit.

Reverend Winter. I'll do that. It will probably be late in the fall.

Chair Eagles. Yes, Mrs. Bastrap.

Mrs. Bastrap. Dr. Hammer, my name is Alexa Bastrap and I am President of the Stonewood College National Alumni Association. The alumni are very concerned about the school being on probation. What will you do different from what the last president did?

Dr. Hammer. At this time I cannot make a distinction between our strategies and those of the previous president. I will be definitive in the plan that I shall present to you in October. I can tell you that we shall address each item cited by the Atlantic Association. In the report that we shall submit to Atlantic we shall show that each issue has been solved or resolved.

Mrs. Bastrap. So you are going to be able to succeed where others have failed?

Dr. Hammer. Mrs. Bastrap, I would say that we, all of us together, are going to succeed.

Chair Eagles. Dr. Hammer, Do you have any questions for us?

Dr. Hammer. Are there any problems at the college, which are not set forth in the reports that I have received? Are there any surprises?

Chair Eagles. We have shared with you everything. You have been given all relevant reports. Additionally, our discussions today and during negotiations of your contract, and during your interview were open and candid. I know how important it is for you to have complete information so that your decisions are well founded. Any leader will look incompetent if he bases decisions on incomplete information. Yes, Reverend Raymondale.

Reverend Raymondale. I am Reverend Justin Raymondale. You remember me from your visit and interviews. I serve as the senior pastor at Cadmount Baptist Church. Dr. Hammer this is a good beginning. You have all the facts and you know what is to be achieved. We stand prepared to assist you.

Chair Eagles. On that note I think that we should bring this meeting to a close. I know that Dr. Stan Zillamen, the vice president for academic affairs is waiting outside to escort the president into a meeting with his cabinet. May I have a motion for adjournment?

Reverend Raymondale. I so move.

Dr. Blakemon. Second.

Chair Eagles. All in favor say Aye.

Aye!

Chair Eagles. Those who oppose say Nay.

Chair Eagles. We stand adjourned. The next meeting is scheduled for October 20th and 21st.

As the light dims on the boardroom a person emerges through a wall on the right side of the room. A spotlight shines on him and he speaks.

I am Dean Waverly Bennings. I served as dean of the faculty from 1920 until 1960. I passed to the other side in 1965. Did you follow the conversation of the trustees? The doubt, the pessimism about the future is remarkable.
They don't seem to know who we are. Imagine if they had been around in 1920. Either you have the commitment or you don't. They lack authenticity. Authentic black men and women know our struggle – don't expect it to be easy and are committed to preserving what was given to them.

We would not have allowed a resource problem to limit the future. If we were like these trustees, Stonewood would not exist today. Their skepticism, their reservation, and their uncertainty constitute a travesty. When I became dean the Atlantic Association would not consider Stonewood. In fact, it was not until 1937 when Atlantic created a special category for black institutions that we became eligible to apply for accreditation within the special category. The illogic in having such a category, which embraced segregation, eventually weighed too much for the association to carry. So in 1956, following well behind the Brown decision, the Atlantic Association allowed all higher education institutions in the region to seek accreditation under one set of standards. How can you allow an organization, which has no history of fairness to intimidate and threaten an institution with great and noble work yet to be done?

During my forty years of work at Stonewood, no companies in the South gave any support to us. If a white person in the South gave anything to a black college in those days, the gift came with the stipulation that it could not be acknowledged.

The president was committed to raising the funds needed to balance the budget and he did. We made whatever sacrifice was required. We knew the mission demanded that we give, that we never concede – the stakes were too high. Indeed, how could we do less? How could we face the next generation knowing that we had denied them Stonewood?

The light fades on Dean Bennings and he fades into the wall. The light now moves to Dr. Hammer and Dr. Zillamen.

President Hammer is met by Dr. Zillamen and escorted back into the boardroom, where the cabinet members are waiting. They all rise as President Hammer and Dr. Zillamen enter the room. Mrs. Wynn is also present.

President Hammer. Please be seated. On my arrival earlier today I met my special assistant, Mrs. Wynn. I asked her to join us to take the minutes for this meeting.

Dr. Hammer. Let's begin with introductions. I want you to tell me your name, the highest academic degree you have earned, the institution from which it was obtained, your current position at the college, how long you have been in the position, and putting AACS aside your view on the most pressing problem/issue facing the college.

Dr. Stan D Zillamen. Mr. President, my name is Stan Zillamen. I have a Ph.D. in chemistry from the University of Michigan. I currently serve as vice president for academic affairs. I have been in this position for four years. Prior to this position I served as chair of the chemistry department for fifteen years. The most pressing issue for the college is adequate funding. Without an increase in funding, we cannot maintain many of the academic programs for which we are well known. Our revenue streams have decreased each year during the last five years. We must generate more funding.

Dr. Louis J Tullson. Good afternoon President Hammer, my name is Louis Tullson. I have an Ed.D. in higher education administration from Harvard University. I hold the position of vice president for financial affairs. I have been in this position for two years and prior to this position I was assistant vice president for finance at Tennessee Technical College. The most pressing issue after what Dr. Zillamen described is the negative press and the cloud of doubt it has generated about our future.

Dr. Alma Y Lemon. Good afternoon Dr. Hammer, my name is Alma Lemon and I serve as vice president for student affairs. I have an Ed.D. from Georgia State University. I have been vice president for three years. Prior to my current assignment I taught in the department of curriculum and instruction at Stonewood for ten years. I think that our most pressing problem is enrollment. We were down 200 students last fall and we may drop another 200 this fall. We have admitted some marginal students in the last three years and our retention of first year students has dropped below 70 percent.

Mr. Nathan C. Bessel. Dr. Hammer, my name is Nathan Bessel. I am serving as vice president for operations. I have an MBA from George Washington University. I have been in this position for five years. Before I took on this assignment I worked in finance as the controller for three years and before that as an accountant for six years. My entire career has been spent at Stonewood. The most pressing issue at the college is our failure to adjust to the current set of circumstances. We have continued to act as if we still had 5,000 students and we were receiving the same level of financial support from alumni, friends, and the local business community as ten years ago.

Dr. Hammer. Mrs. Wynn, what about you?

Mrs. Wynn. Sir, I don't usually participate.

Dr. Hammer. I want you to participate in this discussion.

Mrs. Wynn. Yes sir. My name is Lynne Alice Wynn. I am the special assistant to the president. I have a BA degree from Stonewood College in business administration. I have worked at the college for twelve years. I worked in the office of the vice president for academic affairs for seven years. I have been in the president's office for the last five years. The most pressing issue at the college is leadership. No one accepts responsibility for anything. We have people doing whatever they choose without any consequence.

Dr. Hammer. Thanks for your assessments. I accepted the position of president because my assessment of the problems we currently face led me to conclude that they can be successfully resolved. I am certain that we can show financial stability and have accreditation reaffirmed.

We have some major tasks.

* Development of a plan describing how we shall address all the issues now challenging Stonewood. This plan must be completed in eight weeks.

* Development of the report for AACS which is due exactly fourteen months from today.

The plan must clearly address:

- Revenue Increase
- Enrollment Increase
- Generation of positive press
- Improvement in communication with all constituents
- A balanced budget for this year
- Projection of balanced budgets for the next five years
- Removal of existing deficit
- Repayment of existing loan.

The debt and the deficit must be resolved. I have some ideas about how to proceed. At this time we shall begin a thorough analysis of all aspects of our operation. Dr. Zillamen I want to know those major programs, which in the last five years do not have a total of twenty graduates. I want an analysis of our use of part-time and adjunct faculty. I want a report on our use of support staff. What areas or programs in academic affairs are over staffed and understaffed. If you were to cut the faculty by ten percent, a year from now, who would be on that list and why?

Dr. Tullson, I want an analysis of the collection of tuition and fees for the last five years. I want to see our policy on allowing students to register without paying the full amount due. I also want to see our refund policy. I want to review all contracts, food service, bookstore, print/copier store, and any others. I want a report on parking fees and parking fines assessed and collected. I want a payroll audit conducted without announcement, immediately. I want to know about any property owned by the college that is not adjacent to the campus. I want to see the audits for the last five years.

Before I go on let me be clear. My discussions with you are confidential. If you want to depart this administration immediately then violate the confidentiality of my discussions with you. I expect to meet with each of you separately on these assignments. We cannot delay. There can be no excuse. Each assignment must be completed.

Dr. Lemon I want an analysis of enrollment data for the last ten years. I want to know from what states and cities and counties we receive students. I want to know from what high schools we receive students. I want to know about the students who enroll and not just their academic profiles. Do we have a recruitment plan?

Dr. Lemon. No Dr. Hammer we do not.

Dr. Hammer. You will develop one immediately. I want it done by October 1. It must be informed by data. Dr. Lemon, what is the probability that we shall have more than twenty applicants from Chicago this academic year? Well?

Dr. Lemon. I don't know.

Dr. Hammer. Well, how long will it take you to get an answer?

Silence.

Dr. Hammer. Talk to the people in institutional research.

Dr. Lemon. Yes sir.

Dr. Hammer. Also Dr. Lemon, I need to know about athletic expenses and revenue. Consult with Dr. Tullson and use Mr. Bessel if you need assistance.
Mr. Bessel, I want a report on the condition and use of our buildings. Are we adequately staffed in buildings and grounds? I want a report on the feasibility of outsourcing the maintenance of our buildings and grounds.
I want to see the incident reports from campus security for the last academic year. Are we adequately staffed in security? I want to see the policy on the use of campus facilities by outside groups. I am interested in what we charge these groups.

Mr. Bessel. I'll address the assignment sir.

Dr. Hammer. Mrs. Wynn I want a draft of the minutes of this meeting before you leave today. Unless someone has a question or needs a clarification this meeting is over.

The lights darken on the boardroom. The lights pick up Doctors Zillamen and Lemon as the exit by walking forward and turning stage left as seen by the audience. Dr. Tullson and Mr. Bessel exit before them.

Doctors Zillamen and Lemon confer briefly on their way out of the meeting room.

Dr. Lemon. What do you think?

Dr. Zillamen. He seems to know what he wants to do.

Dr. Lemon. Yes, I heard that he has been consulting with some of his friends who work at other schools about what he needs to do.

Dr. Zillamen. That explains it. Because, I didn't think that he had done very much at Yale. Let's hope for the best.

The light brightens on the president's office. Mrs. Wynn knocks and enters the president's office. Dr. Hammer, Jane LaPortier, a reporter with *The Savannah Morning Times* wants to interview you for an article in the Sunday paper.

Dr. Hammer. So soon?

Mrs. Wynn. Yes sir, she is anxious to talk to you.

Dr. Hammer. Good, this may serve to begin the generation of positive press for the college. Go ahead and arrange it for tomorrow morning before ten. By the way get me Reverend Raymondale's phone number.

Mrs. Wynn exits and returns with papers in her hand.

Mrs. Wynn. Here sir is Reverend Raymondale's number. I am placing the minutes in the in-box on your desk.

The president picks up the minutes and glares at them as he dials Reverend Raymondale's number.

Dr. Hammer. Hello Reverend Raymondale.
(Reverend Raymondale can be heard but not seen by the audience.)

Reverend Raymondale. Hello President Hammer. How can I help you?

Dr. Hammer. I would like to meet with the three trustees who resigned from the board. Could you arrange a breakfast meeting for me, you, and the three former trustees at a place where we can have some privacy.

Reverend Raymondale. We can do it at the DC, the Downtown Club. Now the men you want to meet with are David Kensmith of Kensmith Motors, Albert Smallwood of Smallwood Construction, Inc., and Norris Northington of Northington Realty. I will take care of it. Do you have a preferred date or dates?

Dr. Hammer. Yes any morning next week, preferably at 7:30 a.m.

Reverend Raymondale. Consider it done. I'll get back to you by tomorrow. Have a good evening.

The lights dim on the president's office.

Narrator. The following Sunday morning.

The lights brighten on the kitchen of Trustee Rayson. Trustee Rayson places a call from her kitchen to Chairman Eagles. Chairman Eagles can be heard but not seen by the audience.

Mrs. Rayson. Samuel, have you seen the Sunday paper? According to an article by Jane LaPortier we have a savior at Stonewood. The article implies that we are just a bunch of stumbling, bumbling idiots and we needed our savior, Dr Jason Hammer, to deliver us. There are four pictures of Dr. Hammer, one in his office, one in front of the chapel, one in the student center, and one of him looking out across the campus in a Napoleon-like stance. I could not believe it. Why is LaPortier fascinated with this man? He has been here a week and he is the savior of the college? I have worked hard for this school. I am the most influential African American businesswoman in the state. I have given more money to Stonewood than anyone. I have never received that kind of presentation in the press. Have you ever seen four pictures of me in the Sunday paper? How does he show up and instantly become the savior? I think that we have a major problem.

Chairman Eagles. Just calm down. I agree it is way over the top, but it is not negative. It appears the paper is willing to support Dr. Hammer and apparently thinks that his background is what we need. This is not all bad. We just have to be careful and use the support of the press to advance our agenda.

Mrs. Rayson. But Samuel, how could Hammer allow this reporter to portray him as our savior? How could he think this would win the black community? I'll tell you what I think. I think that we've been had, we've been taken. He belongs to them. Somehow we chose the person who is here to do their bidding. He is theirs and this is an indication that they will seek what they have always sought, and that is to control the destiny of this institution.

Chairman Eagles. You have to know that I was also disturbed by the article. We have been working to save Stonewood and suddenly after one week he is the savior. It is unbelievable. We must be vigilant.

Mrs. Rayson. I thought of asking Hammer what the hell he thought he was doing. But then, I thought that he's just going to play innocent. I agree we have to watch everything.

The lights dim on the kitchen of Trustee Rayson as the conversation continues.

Narrator. Two weeks later.

The lights brighten on the president's office.
Mrs. Wynn phones Dr. Hammer.

Mrs. Wynn. Sir, I have Mr. David Kensmith on the line.

Dr. Hammer. Please put him through.

Dr. Hammer. Hello Mr. Kensmith. It's good to hear from you so soon after our breakfast meeting.
(Mr. Kensmith can be heard but not seen by the audience.)

Mr. Kensmith. Dr. Hammer all of Savannah is impressed with what you have brought to our city – the potential to revive Stonewood. You asked us to think about returning to the board. We have met and discussed the pros and cons and regrettably we have to say no at this time. We do want to help you. At the last meeting of the League to Advance Savannah we decided that a member of the league could help you in dealing with our business community. We want to recommend to you that Jackson Robert Stanmore, who works for the President of the League, become a member of your board. He could help you with understanding city politics, and give advice about fundraising. We think that J Robert could be a real asset to you. And just by having him, you would instantly have the support of the league.

Dr. Hammer. Mr. Kensmith I know from experience that the return of you, Mr. Sandlewood, and Mr. Northington to the board would impress AACS and a host of potential donors. It would convey that the most prominent business leaders in the city believe in the college and support it. Your return would lift us.

Mr. Kensmith. Dr Hammer, that is not going to happen, not anytime soon. The offer of J Robert to work with you and serve on your board has the backing of the most prominent business people in the city. You should not overlook that fact. Additionally, this offer is made because we are impressed with you and we are committed to helping you. It is important that you understand the source of this offer, this opportunity. Remember, you contacted us and we are proposing how we can help you. A negative response to the league does not play well in this city.

Dr. Hammer. Thank you Mr. Kensmith for the generous offer. This will take a few months. Please send me a resume and any relevant background information that you have on Jackson Stanmore.

Mr. Kensmith. I will and I will make certain that J Robert contacts you so that you guys can meet. I think that this will work well for everyone.

Dr. Hammer. I look forward to meeting Mr. Stanmore.

Mr. Kensmith. Good. Well, I've got people waiting. Good-bye.

Dr. Hammer. Good-bye.

The light dims and goes dark on Dr. Hammer. Dean Bennings steps through the right boardroom wall and into the light.

Dean Bennings. Dr. Hammer was never on the street. He should have sidestepped all of that. They sidestepped his request; he should have sidestepped their offer. He was gutted in that conversation. Now the league will control him through Stanmore. Stanmore will report everything that the president plans or openly contemplates. President Hammer has only been at the college a few weeks and he has managed to limit his options. Sadly, he probably doesn't understand it. In fact, he might interpret his relationships with the press and the league as progress. Apparently, he does not realize that his positive press would not have occurred without the a priori blessing of the league. Let's hope that Dr. Hammer learns quickly the importance of protecting his options. Or to put it another way, let's hope he learns to hold his cards close to his vest.

The lights on Dean Bennings dim and he fades into the right boardroom wall.
The lights brighten on the president's office.

Narrator. In mid August just ten days before the college opens for the fall term,
President Hammer calls Chairman Eagles from his office phone.

Chairman Eagles can be heard but not seen by the audience.

Chairman Eagles. Hello, Attorney Eagles speaking.

Dr. Hammer. Good Morning Mr. Eagles. I call to make a special request. During the past few weeks the vice presidents and their staffs have been engaged in extensive reviews. We have found some information that needs to be shared with the full board.

Chair Eagles. Can it wait until the October meeting?

Dr. Hammer. Mr. Chairman, our timeline is quite short. We cannot afford to delay in communicating with you and the board.

Chair Eagles. Just what have you found that warrants a call meeting of the board?

Dr. Hammer. We have found payroll irregularities – people on the payroll who never showed for work at the college. We have found that students last year were exploited by drug dealers and pimps. We have also found that land owned by the college was sold about ten years ago without documented board approval. These are serious matters, which we feel compelled to discuss with the board.

Chair Eagles. You are correct. We need a call meeting of the board. We need to understand what has occurred and determine the damage we have suffered. I know that school opens next week; however, given the seriousness of your findings, we will schedule the meeting for next Tuesday evening at 6 p.m.

Dr. Hammer. Thank you. Of course it will be a single item agenda – a special report by the president.

Chair Eagles. Good. I will inform the board members. See you Tuesday. Good-bye.

Dr. Hammer. Good-bye.

The lights dim on the president's office. After a minute the lights brighten on the boardroom.
Narrator. The following Tuesday the board convenes in the boardroom. Dr. Martin Melvins and Reverend Belvin Winter are absent and participate via phone conference.

Chair Eagles. The meeting of the Board of Trustees of Stonewood College will come to order. This is a call meeting of the board with a one-item agenda – a special report by President Hammer. Since Dr. Melvins is participating via phone conference, I ask Mrs. Rayson to take the minutes. Since those present signed the attendance sheet we will dispense with calling the roll. Let the record show that Dr. Melvins and Reverend Winter are participating via phone conference.

Dr. Hammer the floor is yours.

Dr. Hammer. Mr. Chairman and members of the board, members of my administrative team and I have during the last four to six weeks examined records and data related to our operation. We conducted a payroll audit of the classified staff members who are paid every two weeks. We discovered that twelve persons were on our payroll, who did not work on the campus. We found that the director of buildings and grounds had been collecting the checks for these individuals and then distributing them. He received a 50 percent kick back from each person. We have terminated the director and the twelve individuals.

Chair Eagles. Has this matter been reported to the police?

Dr. Hammer. No, I thought the negative press could be detrimental to our efforts to portray a well-managed institution. If the board wants us to pursue criminal charges against the former director and the twelve individuals who knew that they were involved in a criminal scheme to steal money from the college, we will.

Chair Eagles. I do not favor such an action.

Trustee Rayson. I agree with the chairman. It is good that we caught this. Dr. Hammer do you have any idea about how long this criminal activity has been in operation?

Dr. Hammer. At least two years at the current level. We were able to interview two of the participants who believed that they had done nothing wrong. In fact, they thought the former director is a real crook. He had promised them a larger percentage of each check when they were recruited. He would meet them each payday at a local nightclub. Each individual would endorse his/her check over to the director and he would pay him/her in cash. We think that it started about four years ago with the former director recruiting four persons to participate. After getting away with it for approximately two years the former director recruited more participants.

Trustee Melvins. (Via phone conference) Mr. President, I want to congratulate you on an excellent job in correcting this very bad situation. I have some reservations about not reporting this matter to the police. What are the chances that it will become known?

Dr. Hammer. I share your reservations. I am also aware that given who we are the Atlantic Association is likely to use the incident as the pretext for a visiting committee to probe a wide variety of things associated with our operation. There already exists in the local community, largely due to negative press, the notion that wrongdoing is commonplace at Stonewood.

Chair Eagles. I think that I understand what is at risk here and I do not think that this matter should ever be discussed again. I also think that the minutes should mention only that Dr. Hammer has made personnel changes and recommends that we approve the termination of the director and the twelve staff members. Their names will appear in the minutes. May I have a motion?

Dr. Blakemon. Mr. Chairman, I move approval of the termination of the staff members in buildings and grounds as recommended by President Hammer.

Trustee Melvins. I second that motion.

Chair Eagles. It has been moved and seconded that the board approve the termination of the director of buildings and grounds and twelve staff members as named by President Hammer. Are you ready for the question? All those in favor of the motion please say Aye.

AYE.

Chair Eagles. Opposers please say nay.

Silence.

Chair Eagles. The motion is unanimously approved.

Dr. Hammer. Trustees we have examined records of criminal behavior on the campus last year. We have also interviewed members of our security staff concerning problems experienced last year. We discovered that local drug dealers and pimps had access to our dormitories last academic year. We also learned that during summer school a few of these undesirables were escorted off campus. We are not the first institution to have these problems. It is imperative, however, that we eradicate them on the Stonewood campus. With the savings from the terminations in buildings and grounds we have added three additional security officers and we have hired a new chief of campus security. Information on these individuals is found in the packets in front of you. I realize that these personnel matters would normally be presented at the October meeting; however, our situation requires a record of strong and decisive management. I will guarantee to you and the parents of our students that pimps will not walk the halls of our dormitories soliciting young women to work for them. I will also guarantee that drugs will not be sold on our campus. The four individuals that we recommend to you have experience and backgrounds in campus police work.

Trustee Rayson. I had no idea that such activities were taking place at Stonewood. How do you think that these things could have gone on at Stonewood without our knowledge?

Dr. Hammer. I can only speculate. The chief whose demotion I am recommending has only been on the job for one year. His background is not strong. He was expelled from the local police academy. We had thought that some members of the security force had been bribed; however, we have no evidence. In general, we have found that the force members did not take pride in their work. We have also observed that many of them are physically unfit. I can assure you that the person that we are recommending as the new chief, Richard Irons, will insist on physical fitness, clean and well fitted uniforms, timeliness, and high standards of professional and personal conduct. He understands the challenges we face. I recommend approval of the package of personnel changes found in your packets.

Trustee Raymondale: I so move.

Trustee Winter. (Via phone conference) Second.

Chair Eagles. Are you ready for the question?
All those in favor, please say Aye.

AYE.

Chair Eagles. Those opposed, please say nay.

Silence.

Chair Eagles. The motion is approved. Please continue Dr. Hammer.

Dr. Hammer. Members of the board, the next and final matter is quite perplexing. We found that the college received a gift of ten acres of land about twenty-five years ago on the south side of the city. A portion of Vine Plaza Mall now occupies that land. The land was apparently sold about ten years ago to unknown parties and then sold to a local developer, and sold again to the Brown Corporation. The developer died about six years ago. Our records are incomplete and strangely the real estate records of the city for the transactions are missing. We have searched board minutes and college records and we have not found any evidence that the board ever approved the sale of that land. We have also determined that no funds from the sale were ever received by the college. Why was the land sold? Who approved the sale? What was the selling price? Who purchased the land? We have run into a stonewall in trying to answer these questions. We do know that two former Stonewood board members are members of the board of directors of the Brown Corporation. The Brown Corporation has extensive land holdings around the city.

This is disappointing since it appears that board members may have conspired to use their positions to steal from the college. You recall how zealous law enforcement was in the pursuit of former President Foucault over the allegation that thousands of dollars had been stolen. The land in question was sold to the Brown Corporation for twenty-five million dollars. If the sale of that land involved any board members, the board was guilty of malfeasance and racketeering. If the board was not involved in any manner then the board may have been guilty of gross neglect. Another dimension to this travesty is that long after the land was sold the college's records show it as an asset. It was during the trial and subsequent resignation of Dr. Foucault that the land disappears from documents.

Members of the board, this matter is one that could destroy our efforts to obtain reaffirmation of accreditation.

Chair Eagles. I think that the land was stolen without knowledge by some former board members. I also think that it was done with the help of people who were probably bought off. I do not believe that anyone now on the board conspired to defraud the college. I know that President Foucault would never have participated in such deception. In fact, the record will show that right after Dr. Foucault was replaced we requested of the new president that the record be corrected to show our ownership of land on the south side of the city. I suspect that so many other issues came to occupy the administration that the land simply slipped into the background.

Trustee Melvins. So what action do you propose we take. I feel that there are people in this community who think that they can do anything they choose for or against Stonewood without consequences to them.

Trustee Rayson. Well, Dr. Melvins, what do you want to do? Keep in mind that the sale took place many years ago. Some people would argue that we want someone to pay for the fact that we were sleep at the wheel.

Trustee Melvins. Sleep at the wheel or not is irrelevant, crimes were committed. What do we now do about it?

Chair Eagles. We must not give the Atlantic Association a reason to withdraw our accreditation. We must not initiate actions that could jeopardize the future of the college. I refuse to preside over the closing of Stonewood. There are doors in this community that were once open to us, albeit for the wrong reason, which I believe we can restore.

Trustee Winter. (Via phone conference) Ladies and gentlemen, it seems to me that there is a thirteenth member of this board who influences every argument, every discussion, and every presentation. Any action taken or contemplated acknowledges this board member. This member sways our thinking and corrupts our independence. When actions are considered, we don't begin with what is moral or just; we don't begin with what is in the best interest of our students; and we don't begin with what is legal. Consistently, we yield to the thirteenth member; we yield to the Atlantic Association. Now, I'm not saying that there is no overlap in these perspectives. I am saying that we cannot be intimidated by Atlantic. Our past actions may not have always been fair, or just, or moral, but that does not prevent us from striving to do what is right. We must stand for what is right; otherwise, we forfeit our responsibility as leaders of this college.

Trustee Raymondale. Yes sir, I applaud everything you said. I think that at the right moment we expose the land swindle, but this is not that time. Never forget that we must live in this community.

Chair Eagles. We cannot have knowledge of a crime and then decide that we will report it at some later time. If we do not report this to law enforcement immediately, then we can never report it.

Dr. Hammer. Mr. Chairman, are you concerned about the open phone lines?

Chair Eagles. No, I am not concerned. I am certain that the principals involved in this land deal realized that it would one day come to light. They probably have a plan of action including controlling all the parties who might become involved.

Trustee Rayson. I move that we accept the third part of the president's report as information, lacking sufficient documentation to warrant or justify any action at this time.

Trustee Raymondale. Second

Chair Eagles. Are you ready for the question?
All those in favor, please say aye.

Aye.

Chair Eagles. Opposers, please say nay.

Nay.

Chair Eagles. The Chair hears a nay from Reverend Winter and Dr. Blakemon. The motion is approved. Dr. Hammer, is there more to report or discuss?

Dr. Hammer. We have concluded our report.

Chair Eagles. Then, this meeting is adjourned.

The lights dim on the boardroom as the trustees exit.

Dean Bennings steps through the imaginary right wall of the boardroom and into the light.

Dean Bennings. I was rather proud of Reverend Winter. The others could not hear him. Sadly, they don't see that they have options. Well the semester is underway. Of course the enrollment is down as projected. The president has come under the influence of the league and some board members are petty. The future of the college is more uncertain today than it was when I became dean. The current leaders don't understand the complexity of the problems they face. If only they could resolve who is for them, who is against them, and who just doesn't give a damn, then they could realistically approach the future. At this time there are many members of the community who would like for Stonewood to fade away. It holds stories that some persons would not like told. I am not surprised that Atlantic has sought every opportunity to challenge the continued existence of the HBC's.

The road ahead has never looked less promising.

The lights dim as Dean Bennings fades into the boardroom wall. After a minute the lights brighten on the boardroom.

Narrator. In a cabinet meeting in mid September President Hammer addresses his vice presidents.

Dr. Hammer. We have come a long way in a short time. We have a better understanding of the issues that we face and we have taken some important steps to improve the college. We have control of the campus. No one enters without proper identification or purpose. We are not using part-time faculty except in one department – music. The grounds look good and the buildings are being well maintained. We have improved collection of money owed by international students by informing them in early July that they would not be allowed to register without paying their bills in full. Vice President Zillamen has made certain that all students in classes are properly registered. Our recruitment plan is almost complete.

We face some larger issues. One is the money owed by the college to the Department of Education. Vice President Tullson please explain this debt.

Dr. Tullson. Well, former President Foucault planned for a campus of 7,000 students. He convinced the federal government to lend the college about 25 million dollars to build several dormitories. Six were built and today five of those buildings are vacant. With the drop in enrollment, we are not likely to use the facilities anytime in the near future. As you can understand, we are currently having difficulty servicing the debt. For the last five years the debt has been growing and today stands at 20 million dollars. We are overbuilt. We shall not stand a chance with Atlantic with this growing debt and a declining revenue stream.

Dr. Hammer. What do you think we should do about this problem?

Dr. Zillamen. Mr. President no one is going to give us money to address a debt. We cannot ask for money for that purpose. In fact, to ask would damage our credibility. Only the federal government is in a position to help us.

Dr. Hammer. I agree. The challenge is framing a proposition that yields for us and the government a result that benefits everyone.

Dr. Lemon, what have you learned about the changing demographics in the city?

Dr. Lemon. Dr. Hammer, the fastest growing population of students is Hispanic. Those who go to college locally, enroll at Eastern Georgia Community College.

Dr. Hammer. Is this a population that we should target?

Dr Lemon. Perhaps. EGCC does not have dorms and has been looking for an apartment building to lease or purchase. The leadership at EGCC has stated in the local paper that with residential facilities EGCC could become the largest community college in the state.

Dr. Hammer. That's interesting. I have an invitation from the President of EGCC to have lunch one day next week. Now, Dr. Lemon, are we developing strategies for recruiting Hispanic students?

Dr. Lemon. Sir, I thought that we might need board approval to go in such a direction. We have a few Hispanic students currently; however, we have never openly recruited them.

Dr. Zillamen. I agree that such a strategy toward increasing the enrollment is plausible, perhaps even prudent; however, the board would likely want Dr. Lemon's head on a platter if we pursued this without approval.

Dr. Hammer. Very well, we'll make a presentation to the board on the viability of such a strategy. Dr. Zillamen and Dr. Lemon I want you to prepare and make the presentation at the October board meeting. Are you clear on what I want?

Dr. Zillamen. Yes sir.

Dr. Lemon. Yes Dr. Hammer

Dr. Hammer. I will meet with you about two weeks before the meeting to review the presentation. Concerning the debt, Dr. Tullson will travel to Washington next week to discuss our financial situation and the debt with senior Department of Education officials. I really want us to have some solutions to put on the table at the October board meeting. I have reviewed the grants we have received in the last ten years and we are far from competitive. Dr. Zillamen, I noticed that only Dr. Rama Mahendra has consistently brought in funds through grants. He seems to have a real pipeline in the Department of Education's Science Improvement Program. In fact, all of his grants come from the Department of Education. I would like to talk to him. Perhaps, we can learn something that would help our future financial situation.

On a different topic, I expect to propose to the board that a new member be added. As you know, we will need strong support from the downtown business community when we send our report to AACS. I believe that a man who has been recommended to me can help us with local companies and corporations. I have discussed the merits of this individual joining the board with Chairman Eagles. Recently, I sent his material to the membership committee. I'll share more on this person at a later time. Let's get to work.

The lights grow dim on the boardroom.

Narrator. The next afternoon.

The president is in his office working. The lights grow bright on the president's office. Mrs. Wynn calls him on the intercom.

Mrs. Wynn. Dr. Mahendra is here to see you.

Dr. Hammer. Show him in my office.

Dr. Mahendra. Good afternoon Mr. President, sir.

Dr. Hammer. Good afternoon and please take a seat. I wanted to meet with you because I am impressed with your success at grant writing. You are currently chair of the department of physics. Last year we only had one graduate in physics, the year before that we had two and before that we had zero. How do you account for these low numbers?

Dr. Mahendra. Mathematics, mathematics. The students have very poor mathematics skills. When they arrive at the college, most of them are not prepared to take calculus. Some of them must take developmental education courses. The deficiencies in mathematics eliminate physics as a major.

Dr. Hammer. And, what have you done about this situation?

Dr. Mahendra. Yes, in my latest grant I have a program called the Boundary Constraint Method.

Dr. Hammer. This is some mathematics theory?

Dr. Mahendra. Oh, no sir it is psychology. The focus is on control, and management of the student's environment.

Dr. Hammer. Have you tried this approach before this year?
Dr Mahendra. Yes sir.

Dr. Hammer. And what were the results?

Dr. Mahendra. They were not very good.

Dr. Hammer. Given the low graduation rate in physics and given that the Boundary Constraint Method has not shown itself to be successful in our environment, what accounts for the funding of your last grant?

Dr. Mahendra. My colleagues on the review panel know that the problem is difficult, and they know us.

Dr. Hammer. I see. Would you drop off to Mrs. Wynn a copy of the proposal?

Dr. Mahendra. I will do that today.

Dr. Hammer. When you submitted your proposal, did you know that you would have colleagues on the panel selected to review it?

Dr. Mahendra. Yes sir. The panels are always drawn from science, engineering and mathematics faculty at the HBC's.

Dr. Hammer. Is there a chance that the program staff at the Department of Education would review the work of a panel?

Dr. Mahendra. Oh, those persons are very nice, but they wouldn't know a scalar from a vector.

Dr. Hammer. I see. I noticed that in many of our grants, including yours, the indirect costs are very low and in some cases zero. Do you understand why this is occurring?

Dr. Mahendra. In some cases, the grant programs that focus on human development limit the amount that can be requested for indirect costs. In others, we elect not to request indirect costs in order to make our grant applications more competitive.

Dr. Hammer. So we discount our services and facilities, though we are in great need of an increase in revenue.

Dr. Mahendra. I never thought of it that way.

Dr. Hammer. I am curious about the small number of graduates in mathematics. What do you tell the freshmen who have interest in mathematics?

Dr. Mahendra. We are honest. We tell them that mathematics is difficult and that most of them will decide to major in some other field.

Dr. Hammer. Do you think that your message discourages the students from making an effort?

Dr. Mahendra. No sir. We are just honest.

As he rises from his chair, the president speaks.

Dr. Hammer. Thank you Dr. Mahendra. This has been informative and helpful.

Dr Mahendra rises and shakes the president's hand as he exits the door.

The lights on the president's office dim and then brighten.

Narrator. Later that evening the president calls Dr. Zillamen from his office phone.

Dr. Zillamen is heard by the audience but not seen.

Dr. Zillamen. Hello, the Zillamen residence.

Dr. Hammer. Stan, hello. This is Jason Hammer.

Dr. Zillamen. Good evening sir.

Dr. Hammer. I just read the latest funded proposal from Dr. Mahendra. It is poorly written. It is so poorly done that if it were shared with anyone we would be embarrassed. The document is incoherent. It is difficult to understand how it could have been funded.

Dr. Zillamen. We have known for sometime that the funding decisions in that program were based only on personal connections with the review panel. If someone other than Dr. Mahendra had submitted that proposal, it would have been rejected.

Dr. Hammer. Well, we have enough problems. We do not have the time to address those in the Science Improvement Program at the U. S. Department of Education. Have a good evening and I'll see you tomorrow. Good-bye.

Dr. Zillamen. Good-bye.

The lights on the president's office dim. After a minute the lights grow bright again.

A few days later Dr Hammer answers the intercom in his office.

Dr. Hammer. Yes Mrs. Wynn.

(Mrs. Wynn is heard but not seen.)

Mrs. Wynn. Dr. Hammer, Dr. Lemon arranged for you to meet with the student government leaders. The meeting is on your calendar for this morning.

Dr. Hammer. Yes. Are they here?

Mrs. Wynn. Yes sir. I put them in the boardroom.

The lights dim on the president's office and grow bright on the boardroom.

The president enters the boardroom and five students rise to greet him.

Dr. Hammer. Good morning. I had wanted to meet with you earlier, but my schedule has been demanding. I have been informed by Dr. Lemon about your activities and your plans for this academic year. Before we address any issues, please introduce yourselves to me.

Mr. Marcus Turnipseed. Dr. Hammer, my name is Marcus Turnipseed. I am the student government association president. I am a senior political science major from Augusta, Georgia.

Ms. Tameka Kellogan. Dr. Hammer, my name is Tameka Kellogan. I am the SGA vice president. I am a junior marketing major from Columbia, South Carolina.

Ms. Skyla Renee Dickenson. Good morning Dr. Hammer, my name is Skyla Renee Dickenson. I am serving as the SGA secretary. I am a junior English major from Savannah.

Mr. Devarious Watersmith. Dr. Hammer, my name is Devarious Watersmith. I am the SGA treasurer. I am a senior sociology major from Atlanta.

Ms. Kyla Anne Author. Good morning Dr. Hammer, my name is Kyla Anne Author. I am the SGA parliamentarian. I am a senior business administration major from Baton Rouge, Louisiana.

Dr. Hammer. Great. Tell me why you chose to attend Stonewood.

Ms. Author. I don't have a problem with going first. I am here because my parents are friends of Reverend Belvin Winter. Reverend Winter talked about what a great place this is. I think that he had convinced all of us that Stonewood was the best place for me by my junior year in high school.

Mr. Turnipseed. I came to Stonewood because my parents attended Stonewood and they told me that I could go anywhere I wanted to go as long as it was Stonewood. I never thought about attending another college.

Mr. Watersmith. My situation is the same as Marcus. Since my parents attended and met here, I always thought that Stonewood is where I belong.

Ms. Kellogan. Well, my parents did not attend Stonewood, but one of my aunts did and she wanted me to attend. She has paid my tuition each semester since I entered the college.

Ms. Dickenson. I also am part of a legacy. My maternal grandmother attended Stonewood. She did not pressure me to attend, but she was so happy when she learned that I had chosen Stonewood.

Dr. Hammer. Thank you for sharing that information. As you know the college has been adjusting to a large enrollment decline for the last two years. I was curious about the reasons you chose Stonewood. As we develop strategies to reverse the decline in enrollment, we must take advantage of the reasons that students currently attend. Let's now focus on issues and questions you wish to raise.

Mr. Turnipseed. Thank you Dr. Hammer. It's an honor to meet you. We are grateful for this meeting and for your contributions to Stonewood. We hear rumors everyday that the college is unaccredited, or that we just lost accreditation. Sir, just what is our status?

Dr. Hammer. We are accredited by the Atlantic Association of Colleges and Schools. Currently, we are on probation because the Association has found evidence that we do not meet the standard for financial stability. We are working each day to improve our financial stability and to demonstrate to Atlantic that we meet the financial stability standard. We must submit a report next September, approximately a year from now, to Atlantic setting forth our case that Stonewood is financially stable. Subsequently, at its December meeting, Atlantic will take one of four possible actions: reaffirm accreditation, upgrade us to warning, continue us on probation, or remove our accreditation status. The college has not lost its accreditation and remains eligible to participate in all federal grant programs. Some of you should know this. Do any of you receive federal financial aid?

Mr. Turnipseed. Yes, I do.
Ms. Dickenson. I do.
Mr. Watersmith. Yes sir I receive aid.
Ms. Author. Yes.

Dr. Hammer. So everyone but Ms. Kellogan. If we were unaccredited, then you would not be able to receive federal financial aid.

Ms. Author. Dr. Hammer, many colleges and universities have coed residential halls.
Why can't we have coed dormitories at Stonewood?

Dr. Hammer. We could have coed dormitories if the board of trustees were to approve them. The current residential options on our campus are limited and would probably be regarded by many of our students as conservative and traditional. Many of our constituents would not support any change in our housing policies. If you want to change the residential policies on the campus, you will need to petition the board for permission to conduct a referendum on the proposed change. If the referendum yields support for the change, then that would become a significant element in the proposal that you would prepare for submission to the board. I urge you to discuss this matter with Dr. Lemon. She can guide you in preparation of the petition.

Ms. Author. If the students vote in favor of coed residential halls, will you support the proposal that will go to the board?

Dr. Hammer. I will. You should keep in mind that a close positive vote is a vote for the status quo. You will need a positive vote of at least 70 percent of those voting and you will need a turn out of slightly more than 70 percent of the student population. To obtain such a turn out is a major challenge, since less than 40 percent of our students vote in campus elections.

Ms Dickenson. Dr. Hammer, one of the issues that students talk about is that tuition and fees continue to increase. The cost to attend Stonewood is more than twice the cost of attending the University of Savannah (US). The facilities at US are better and coed dormitories are available. It seems to me that if we were serious about being competitive, then we would not cling to outdated practices and policies. What are you planning to do about maintaining or even reducing the cost of attending Stonewood? You must realize that federal financial aid burdens us with debt that places us in bondage before we have the opportunity to begin our careers. Thus, it is reasonable to attend the school with the lowest cost.

Dr. Hammer. Ms. Dickenson you make some excellent points. Let me begin by pointing out that there are many dimensions to a college education. First and foremost is the opportunity to pursue the major discipline of your choice. Now we don't have an engineering program at the college; however, if you express to the Stonewood faculty that you want to become an engineer, your choice will be affirmed and embraced with support. If you attended US, which has an engineering program, your choice would not be affirmed and embraced. In fact, you would have to prove that you have the background and the ability to pursue engineering. Your decision would be greeted with skepticism, and doubt, even discouragement. The opportunity for students to pursue any field of study without clouds of doubt about their abilities is the challenge that the existence of the HBC's has made to higher education in America.

As Dr. Hammer pauses, the lights on him dim and brighten on Dean Bennings who has emerged from the right imaginary wall of the boardroom.

Dean Bennings. It is an extraordinary challenge, because of the biases that so many of the learned and the unlearned hold about who can achieve and even who deserves the opportunity to achieve. If you happen to need a second chance to show that you have acquired the knowledge and the skills associated with topics in a given subject, that chance is fundamental to our approach to education. At US the approach taken would deny you that chance. The approach taken is to find a way to eliminate you, not necessarily based on race, but based on the notion that only certain individuals can be successful in engineering. At Stonewood, your personhood is recognized. You can participate in any activity. You are not limited by stereotypes. You want to play golf, or go out for the cheerleader squad, or the debate team – these options are yours. I don't think that the US has had an African, or a Hispanic American woman as Miss US. Stonewood has always embraced a pluralistic society. Because of its ideals, its philosophy, and its history Stonewood's future should be secure. How could the nation not embrace Stonewood?

The lights dim on Dean Bennings as he recedes into the imaginary right wall. The lights brighten on Dr. Hammer.

Dr. Hammer. Now, about the increasing cost of education, I agree that the financial aid system leaves many of our students with a mountain of debt. As an educational institution, we should be declared an ineffective institution because of the debt that our graduates have. Of course, this concept does not exist among the standards and criteria of the regional accrediting associations. We must discourage our students from borrowing money that is used to afford them a more comfortable life style. Now as a college, we need to provide some leadership in assisting our students with reducing their reliance on federal financial aid. At some institutions, Stonewood included, the cost of taking courses in the summer is cheaper. Also, students have the flexibility of taking some courses during the summer at other colleges. By shopping around a student could save money. Also by attending continuously, which means taking courses in summer school, a student could easily finish in three years. Financial aid counseling should not be about obtaining the maximum loan, but about assisting the student in reaching his/her goal with minimum debt. That might mean a six-year plan as opposed to a four-year one and it might include some employment. The main point is that we have to give our students a better financial opportunity when they graduate than we currently do. It will be difficult to reduce our costs. Currently, over 80 percent of our expenses are in salaries and benefits. Later this academic year we shall examine our organizational structure with an objective of reducing redundancy. We want to be lean and efficient. We may look at some older models, which did not have a vice president for every major organizational division. Our aim will be to minimize the salaries and benefits for the administration. We may give some faculty members reduced teaching loads in order to assign them some administrative functions. For example, the study abroad director's position, which is vacant, will probably not be filled. We shall assign the responsibilities to one or two faculty members in the department of foreign languages. We must find support from the foundation community and wealthy individuals to aid us in making scholarships available.

The lights on Dr. Hammer dim and brighten on Dean Bennings as he emerges from the right wall of the boardroom.

Dean Bennings. To keep the spectrum of educational institutions in America very broad with different histories, different missions, and different philosophies, is in the interest of a creative and vibrant society. We must take steps to remain competitive. What do we offer a prospective student to compete with the lower cost of the US? Do we offer scholarships, the success of our graduates in the academic discipline in which the student is interested, or aspects of our history and mission, or some combination of these? I think that we use everything. We cannot compete with Harvard, Stanford, and the University of Chicago in science and technology, but in the quest for the advancement of civil rights and human rights the historically Black colleges have inspired persons around the planet. We can offer students an education in the crucible of a philosophy, a mission fashioned by the painful pursuit of a better America – in pursuit of what Langston Hughes eloquently captured with the poem, "Let America Be America."

The lights dim on Dean Bennings as he fades into the right wall. The lights again brighten on Dr. Hammer.

Ms. Dickenson. Thank you Dr. Hammer. I am glad that you are our leader.

Mr. Turnipseed. Last academic year we had several persons on the campus at night selling drugs. Some women complained repeatedly about being approached and even coerced into working as prostitutes. What have you done to improve safety on campus?

Dr. Hammer. I am surprised that you have not already been informed about the changes we have made in campus security. We have hired a new chief of campus security, Chief Richard Irons, and three new security officers. We have secured all entrances and exits to the campus. Officers are on duty at all entrances 24 hours per day. The campus is patrolled continuously. Our officers are involved in training seminars that focus on all aspects of their work. They also are involved in physical training each day to ensure that that they are sufficiently fit to meet the responsibilities of the work. We are serious about campus safety. We have discussed the problems that occurred last year with the local police and we have their cooperation in protecting the students at Stonewood from the drug dealers and pimps.

Mr. Watersmith. Dr. Hammer, we have had some of our requests for concerts and outside speakers rejected. Why can't we have the artists and speakers that we choose?

Dr. Hammer. We expect that the choices you make and recommend to me for approval will reflect the interests of all students and not a small minority. We also expect that your choices will not put the college and its constituents at risk. We also examine whether the expense is prudent given that the funding comes from an activity fee paid by all students enrolled. We intend to be supportive; however, we will reject your requests if we determine that they are not in the best interests of the college.

Mr. Turnipseed rises from his seat and the other students follow his lead. Dr. Hammer rises.

Mr. Turnipseed. Thank you Dr. Hammer for addressing our questions and concerns.

Dr. Hammer. Please let me know when you would like to visit again. I am available to all members of the Stonewood community.

As the students leave Mrs. Wynn informs the president that she needs to see him.

Mrs. Wynn. Dr. Hammer, I need to speak with you.

Dr. Hammer. Come right in.

Sir, Ms. LaPortier wants to talk with you about another article focusing on what brought you to Stonewood. She wants to have the article and pictures ready for a Sunday edition of the paper in October.

Dr. Hammer. I don't see how I can say no. Hopefully, this will help build community support for the college. Arrange for me to talk with her early next week.

The lights dim on the boardroom. After a minute the lights brighten on the president's office where Dr. Hammer is working.

Narrator. It is early October and President Hammer has arranged to meet in his office with the leaders of the Stonewood National Alumni Association. They are President Alexa Bastrap, Vice President Walter Shreve, and Secretary Kimberly Castleburg. Mrs. Wynn informs Dr Hammer that they have arrived. She buzzes him on the intercom.

Mrs. Wynn. Dr Hammer, the alumni association officers are here and I have placed them in the boardroom.

Dr. Hammer. Thanks, I'll be there in one minute.

The lights dim on the president's office and brighten on the boardroom.

Dr. Hammer enters the boardroom and the members of the alumni association rise.

Dr. Hammer speaks as he enters and shakes hands.

Dr. Hammer. Good morning, I am delighted to meet with you. You represent one of the pillars of this great institution. As you know, we have some challenges that we are committed to meeting, successfully. I am aware that you wanted to meet with me early in September, and I regret that this is our first opportunity. Please know that I am supportive of you and that I am grateful for your many contributions to the college.

Mrs. Bastrap. Thank you Dr. Hammer. As I entered the campus, I thought that the security officer at the gate was rude to me. He had me wait while he called your office to confirm that I had an appointment. I resented sitting there while he called Mrs. Wynn. Also, as I finally drove through the gate, I noticed quite a bit of paper and other trash on the grounds. These things concern me.

Dr. Hammer. Mrs. Bastrap, they also concern me. Because of our commitment to keep the drug dealers and pimps off this campus, everyone entering the campus is stopped. I shall report to the chief that you felt that the officer was rude. We are sensitive about customer service, and we strive to be friendly, polite, and of service to all persons who have legitimate business at the college. As you know, we have made changes in the leadership of buildings and grounds. I shall report your observations to the superintendent of buildings and grounds. We are determined to have a clean and attractive campus.

Mrs. Bastrap. Well, I hope so. Now, in this town, we don't trust the League to Advance Savannah and we definitely don't trust *The Savannah Morning Times*. I don't know if you know what you are doing by courting these people and currying favor with them. Many of the alumni are concerned, and some are even angry that you seem to be under the influence of people who have shown that they are not our friends. We thought you were the President of Stonewood College, not its savior.

Dr. Hammer. I am aware of the mistrust that exists between some of us and many established organizations in Savannah. I know that the league and *The Savannah Morning Times* have at times taken positions and actions that hurt the college. As President of Stonewood, I must act in its best interest as I am able to understand that interest. Since I arrived, I have sought to build bridges to the business community and gain support for the continued existence of the college. I have sought to position the college so that the leaders of local businesses would feel compelled – would feel an obligation to give to the college. I have not sought a high profile. On the other hand, I have not avoided the press because I want a friendly and supportive relationship with its members. I do not believe that we can achieve reaffirmation of accreditation without the support of all the major institutions in this city. I cannot act in a negative manner, or show hostility to the league or to *The Savannah Morning Times*. To do so would violate the trust that the board has in me to lead successfully all of us on this journey toward reaffirmation of accreditation for Stonewood College.

Mrs. Bastrap. I want you to know that we are suspicious of those people and now we have some doubts about you.

Dr. Hammer. Mrs. Bastrap, I need all of us pulling together on behalf of Stonewood. I need you and the alumni association to stand firm behind the college. We cannot succeed if we have internal strife. Judge me by my actions and what I am able to achieve.

Mr. Shreve. Dr. Hammer, I am Walter Shreve and I serve as vice president of our organization. When I was at Stonewood, I was a Black college All American in football for three years. Then, I went to the NFL where I had a great career – at least that's what the newspapers claim – for ten years. You know that for the last four years, we have won the South Atlantic Athletic Conference in football. Now this year, we have already lost two games. Some of us are very upset about this and think that you should take some action. What are you going to do?

Dr. Hammer. I am aware that football has played a significant role in the history of Stonewood. I know that we hired a new coach prior to the change that the board made in the leadership of the college. As important as winning on the football field on Saturday afternoon is for many of our alumni and fans, it is not our primary focus and cannot become our primary focus.

Mr. Shreve. You must not realize that football made Stonewood and can save Stonewood.

Dr. Hammer. Mr. Shreve, the year we won the conference championship in football the college was placed on warning by the Atlantic Association. Again in a year that we won the conference championship in football, the college was placed on probation. We must keep things in perspective. At this time, you and all our former football stars and former star athletes in other sports can help the college through major gifts to the college and through planned giving. We can send you a brochure with information on a number of ways you can aid in securing the future of Stonewood.

Mrs. Castleburg. Dr. Hammer, my name is Kimberly Castleburg, and I serve as secretary to the national alumni association. In the three months that you have been here, you have not been to one of our events. People are saying that you don't like us. Why don't you attend our events?

Dr. Hammer. Unfortunately, there have been numerous events involving alumni, donors, and general supporters of the college that I have not been able to attend. You should realize that I always send a representative, and I convey my regrets well before the scheduled date for each event. I hope that you understand that because the college is on probation, I must use my time strategically. I must be able to relate the use of my time to obtaining reaffirmation of accreditation for the college. I value the alumni association; I value you, and I am grateful for your support of the college. I will make some of your future events. I have placed the national meeting for next March on my calendar.

Mrs. Bastrap. What are you going to do about all these vacant dormitories on this campus?

Dr. Hammer. We face the challenge of demonstrating to the Atlantic Association that Stonewood is a financially stable institution. During President Foucault's administration, the college built residence halls based on the president's vision of reaching an enrollment of seven thousand students. We are now at about one half of that number. We have a large debt for the construction of those vacant dormitories; a debt, which for several years the college has not serviced. We are exploring alternatives for addressing the debt and for making use of the vacant dormitories. Fortunately, they are in an isolated wing of the campus and are not noticed by visitors.

Mrs. Bastrap. Well, whatever you do, don't disrespect Dr. Foucault.

Mrs. Castleburg. We are concerned about the way the young women on this campus dress. They wear shorts, mini skirts and low-cut halter tops to class and to all college functions. What are you and your administration going to do about it?

Dr. Hammer. I found that some years ago Stonewood had a dress code. It appears that while Dr. Foucault was president that the college relaxed efforts to enforce a dress code. We realize that our students have views of dress and fashion that are very different than what many of us would recommend. Our position is that if it is not lewd, provocative, and/or disruptive, then it is acceptable. We must keep in mind that dress and fashion are continuously changing. We don't want to take positions that we cannot reasonably enforce.

Mrs. Castleburg. I just want to say I know that Dr. Foucault maintained and enforced a dress code on this campus. If Dr. Foucault were still president, young women would not be going to class dressed like hookers on the street. This college has a history of enforcing standards of conduct.

Dr. Hammer. According to what I have read, Dr. Foucault was diligent in the enforcement of standards of conduct for students, faculty and staff during his tenure as president. Members of my staff who worked with Dr. Foucault have informed me that he ceased to enforce the dress code during the last four years of his presidency.
We will not allow dress, which interferes with the normal activities and mission of the college. You should understand that our young women know what the women at the University of Savannah wear. They know what the students at Howard wear. They know what the women at Wellesley and Vassar wear. We live in a connected society; we are not isolated. We cannot afford to be isolated.

Mrs. Castleburg. I don't care about Howard or Vassar. I do care about Stonewood and I think that you and your administration need to do something about the way the women on this campus dress.

Dr. Hammer. I understand your view and your recommendation. I shall share your concerns with my cabinet. I want you to know that we strive to educate our students about the consequences of antisocial behavior and the importance of following accepted societal norms for dress, speech, and general deportment.

Mr. Shreve. Dr. Hammer, I want to go back to the importance of football at Stonewood. We have more former professional football players than any other HBC. These guys have resources that could be shared with the college. I don't think that you should just push football aside.

Dr. Hammer. Mr. Shreve, my earlier comment to you was about maintaining perspective and understanding what is important. It is the case that we have among our alumni many former professional football players. It is also the case that 99 percent of them have never given any money to the college. Other than showing up for football games and a few other athletic events, the overwhelming majority of these men demonstrate no support for the college. They are prepared to offer advice about football, which they do on a regular basis.

Mrs. Bastrap. The most important thing at this time is getting the college off probation. What are you doing to ensure that Stonewood is once again accredited by the Atlantic Association?

Dr. Hammer. We addressed some of what we are doing in the answer to your question about the vacant dormitories on campus. As you know, we are working on a report that will be submitted to Atlantic next September. The report will set forth the case that Stonewood is financially stable. The issues are the debt and our failure to service it for several years, a declining enrollment, the decline in contributions to the college, and the diminished support from local businesses and corporations. We must demonstrate for the coming fiscal year a balanced budget. The vice presidents and I are working on these issues and we expect to present a report that will achieve our objective. We are working with the U. S. Department of Education officials, and several persons in this community to develop viable alternatives for the college to solve its problems. Mrs. Bastrap, as a member of the board, you are informed about our efforts. We shall make important presentations at the upcoming board meeting.

Mr. Shreve. Have you spoken to Dr. Foucault since you became President of Stonewood?

Dr. Hammer. I spoke with Dr. Foucault on my first day at the college. He pledged his support and wished me a successful tenure as president. Unfortunately, I have not had the opportunity to speak with him since then. He is a valuable resource and we will use him when appropriate.

Mrs. Castleburg. What are we doing about the bookstore? I heard that our students couldn't purchase books.

Dr. Hammer. Because the college went through several years of not paying its bills on time, many vendors including the major book publishers, will only work with us if we pay in advance. We have worked with the bookstores at other colleges in the area to sell our students books. Some of the introductory textbooks are the same as the ones being used at other schools. In some cases we have paid in advance for the books ordered. I think that all students have been able to obtain their books. We are in negotiations with American Books, Inc. to operate the bookstore on our campus. We expect to have a contract by next January.

Dr. Hammer. Although I would like to continue our discussion, I have another engagement. Certainly, we can meet as the need arises. Thank you so much for sharing with me your concerns.

Dr. Hammer rises and the officers of the alumni association also rise and move toward the door.

As they exit Mrs. Wynn speaks to Dr. Hammer.

Mrs. Wynn. Sir, Mr. Jackson Stanmore called to say that he cannot meet you at the city club as planned. He wants to come by the office tomorrow at 8:00 a.m.

Dr. Hammer. Very well.

The lights grow dim on the boardroom.

Narrator. The next morning.

The lights grow bright on Dr. Hammer's office where Mr. Stanmore is seated.

Dr. Hammer. Well Jackson, you and I have talked several times and I have shared with you documents to bring you up to speed on our situation.

Mr. Stanmore. Jason, are you certain that the board will approve me as a board member?

Dr. Hammer. Yes, there is no rationale that would justify your rejection.

Mr. Stanmore. I'm glad to hear that. Right now you have the good will of some very important people in this city. We need to build on it and not do anything to jeopardize it. Have you thought about what you would do if this does not work out? This is a good place to live. Over the next few weeks I am going to introduce you to people who can help you no matter what you do in the future.

Dr. Hammer. I have not given much thought to what I will do next. I have been so absorbed with the task in front of me that I haven't thought about what my options would be if we fail to obtain reaffirmation of accreditation. I believe that the board would probably use any set back as a reason to terminate me.

Mr. Stanmore. Exactly. Now that land deal that you discovered had taken place without board approval.

Dr. Hammer. Yes.

Mr. Stanmore. Forget it. You should leave it alone. Its dirty laundry, whose exposure could only embarrass the college and its board. Additionally, it has the potential to upset some people in this community who want to support you. Pursuing it is like throwing rocks in a crowd. You don't know whom you are going to hit.

Dr. Hammer. The board has already been informed about our discovery. The members are likely to press for some type of resolution.

Mr. Stanmore. Trust me. If you don't bring this matter to the table, no one else will. They know that deals were made and that some of them were complicit in some way. Think about it. It is hard to believe that a land deal, which involved land in an area of the city where land values have multiplied in value by a factor of ten, could have occurred without somebody on the board having knowledge. This matter has the potential to damage you and Stonewood.

Dr. Hammer. I understand. I will consider the points you've made.

Mr. Stanmore. Consider the points I've made! Jason, you really don't have an option. Pursue this land deal thing and you will never receive a dime from the business community; pursue it and every institution in this part of the state will turn on you; pursue it and many of your board members will turn against you. There is nothing to consider.

Dr. Hammer. It seems that I am in quicksand.

Mr. Stanmore. Only, if you do the wrong thing.

Dr. Hammer. I got it. Let's talk about the support that we can get from the business community.

Mr. Stanmore. After the upcoming board meeting you should make a presentation to the league. Explain to the members what is at stake and make the case for their support of Stonewood.

Dr. Hammer. This is a campaign to raise funds for the college and to obtain pledges for future support.

Mr. Stanmore. Exactly, and as long as we go about it in the right way we will succeed. My value to you Jason is that I know this community, and I know how to find and obtain its resources.

Dr. Hammer. Jackson, it is clear we are going to need your expertise, my knowledge of higher education and some old fashion luck.

Mr. Stanmore. I am going to have to leave. You can reach me at anytime by getting in touch with my secretary, Margret. Keep me informed and have a great day.

Dr. Hammer. You too. By the way there is going to be another article on me in a Sunday edition of the paper.

Mr. Stanmore. I know. That's good for you and the college. Talk to you soon.

Mr. Stanmore departs and Dr. Hammer slouches in his chair looking perplexed.

A short time later Mrs. Wynn calls Dr. Hammer on the intercom.

Dr. Hammer. Good morning Lynne.

(Mrs. Wynn can be heard but not seen.)

Mrs. Wynn. Good morning sir. Would you like a cup of coffee?

Dr. Hammer. Yes Lynne, thank you.

Mrs. Wynn enters Dr. Hammer's office and places the cup of coffee on his desk.

Mrs. Wynne. Sir the cabinet meeting is at 10 and after that you are free.

Dr. Hammer. The meeting will be long because we are discussing the upcoming board meeting.

Mrs. Wynn. Do you want me in the meeting?

Dr. Hammer. No, continue to work on the letters to local politicians.

Mrs. Wynn. Yes sir.

The lights grow dim in the president's office and bright in the boardroom.
The cabinet meeting has just started and the president is speaking.

Dr. Hammer. I am going to ask a series of questions, which I want us to answer.
What is our recommendation on how to address the 10 million-dollar deficit from last year?

Dr. Tullson. Mr. President our options are limited. We can only recommend that the board approve withdrawing 10 million dollars from the college's endowment. No one is going to help us with this problem. This will essentially eliminate the endowment and put us at considerable risk. We have been struggling with cash flow and will not have any reserve funds in the near future.

Dr. Hammer. Although this is a problem that I found when I arrived, the board will not be pleased with this recommendation.

Dr. Tullson. Well, Dr. Hammer we have some other challenges. I just learned that prior to my arrival that the college failed periodically over a four-year time span to meet its obligation to submit payroll taxes – so-called 941 taxes. Although we have been paying these taxes, the IRS is demanding that we submit payment for all past due taxes. Here is what you must understand. They have taken the payments that we have made and applied them to the past due amount. In effect we are eliminating the liability of past administrations. The person I talked to made it clear that the IRS has been patient long enough. He said that you and I could be held liable for the taxes.

Dr. Hammer. This is a real surprise. How many more can we take? Wouldn't the IRS go after the board members for any monies owed?

Dr. Tullson. It seems reasonable that the board members would be liable. There is some arbitrariness in how the IRS might proceed. A colleague told me about a small school in Texas that had the same problem. After the president and the vice president for finance had departed the IRS chose to go after them. These individuals had paid the 941 taxes while at the school; however, the administration prior to theirs had failed to pay all taxes. The IRS did not go after a single board member and went after the president and vice president who had paid the taxes while at the school. The IRS had taken their payments and applied them to the past due amounts. Thus, the past administration was clear and the individuals who had made payments were now liable for taxes due during their watch.

Dr. Hammer. I don't understand the IRS ignoring the board members of that school.

Dr. Tullson. That decision was probably political. The board probably had very influential people on it. They would not have been easy targets for IRS personnel who expected to live in that community.

Dr. Hammer. We are talking about the IRS.

Dr. Tullson. Sir, we are talking about human beings.

Dr. Hammer. What do we need to be current?

Dr. Tullson. We owe about 2 million dollars to the IRS and we owe retirement contributions of another 2 million dollars. The past due retirement contributions are actually part of the deficit. Dr. Hammer, did the board tell you about this problem?

Dr. Hammer. You already have the answer to that question. So, we have a four million dollar problem. What do we do about this?

Dr. Tullson. Dr. Hammer, given the support that you have from the league, the local IRS office is not going to move on us. We have time to try to remedy the situation.

Dr. Hammer. It is crucial to what we are trying to achieve that no one discusses this matter.

Dr. Tullson. Our failure to make retirement payments is already well known. Faculty members ask each quarter when they receive their statements when we plan to make the deposits to their accounts. AACS knows about the retirement problem but not about our difficulty with the IRS. We have paid the faculty contributions to their respective retirement accounts, but we have not consistently paid our portion.

Dr. Hammer. Well, tell the others here about your visit to Washington.

Dr. Tullson. The Department of Education wants to find a way to help us pay off the loan. The officials with whom I met suggested that they might settle for ten cents on the dollar. They offered no suggestions on how to raise the two million dollars.

Dr. Hammer. Think of it this way. Excluding the deficit that we started the year with we are 22 million dollars in the hole, and we might be able to pull even if we could come up with four million dollars.

Dr. Tullson. Dr. Hammer, our debt is somewhat greater than that.

Dr. Hammer. Yes, I know. Let's talk about what we need to balance the current budget. I understand that it was based on 3,800 students. We have 3,600 and we are likely to drop a few in January. Dr. Tullson, how much do we need to balance this year?

Dr. Tullson. Well, given our current discounts and assuming a loss in enrollment in January of fifty students we would end the year with a deficit of 1.15 million dollars.

Dr. Hammer. Let's summarize. The Department of Education wants out of the housing loan deal as much as we do. It probably makes somebody look very bad to have made such an investment. We have an IRS problem. We are delinquent in submitting retirement funds. We have a potential deficit of 1.15 million dollars for this year. We began the year with a ten million dollar deficit. The current endowment is worth just over ten million dollars.
Let's consider other aspects of our situation. Can we increase our enrollment?

Dr. Lemon. Dr. Hammer we have a negative image. Many people think that we are unaccredited. I have learned from interviewing freshmen that many high school counselors tell their students that we are going to lose accreditation. This behavior is especially prevalent in the state. I have looked at the possibility of attracting Hispanic students. Based on the analysis we did we could in three years have a Hispanic population of one thousand students.

Given that the decline in the enrollment of African American students is likely to continue, the recruitment of Hispanic students would be prudent. In three years our total enrollment could be around four thousand. If we are able to increase our enrollment with Hispanic students, we expect the enrollment of African American students to begin to increase. We expect the enrollment of Hispanic students to stabilize us, and make us more competitive for other populations.

Dr. Hammer. What about January? What can we do to keep from losing any students? If we retain our current students and gain 100 students we would cut the potential deficit in half. Dr. Lemon, at mid-term you must focus the efforts of the retention program on assisting each student who is not doing well academically. Dr. Zillamen will make available some faculty who are willing to make a contribution by working with these students without compensation. The faculty members will have to volunteer to do this. It can be done.

Dr. Lemon. Yes sir, I will take care of it.

Dr. Hammer. And prepare to make a presentation to the board on our plan to recruit Hispanic students. Now, what do we plan to do about fundraising?
I shall take this one.

At the upcoming board meeting the committee on board membership will, based on my recommendation, nominate Mr. Jackson Stanmore for a seat on the board. Mr. Stanmore has been helpful to me and knows how to reach important people in this city. He will be an asset in helping me with fundraising.

Dr. Zillamen. Do we have a goal?

Dr. Hammer. I don't want to establish one for this year. Once I see how the business community responds, then I will be in a position to set a goal for next year informed by history – something AACS will have to acknowledge. We realize that something between 500K and a million dollars would be the level of annual support that we need. Rebuilding the endowment is something we will return to after we get through this difficult period. Mr. Stanmore will work with me on this development project. Although I am comfortable taking the lead on development matters, I welcome his assistance with our business community. I have given some thought to searching for a development officer. Given our circumstance, I have decided to wait.

Now, what can we do to generate more positive press?

Dr. Zillamen. The local press seems to like you. No president in the history of this college has had the kind of positive press you have received. If that continues, the larger community will be influenced. If it were not for the devastation of the public's confidence in any institution that has been placed on warning or probation, our prospects for recovery would be very high. I wonder if the people at AACS realize the damage done to an institution by placing it on probation. Everything that AACS wants the institution to do is made more difficult by placing it on probation.

Once on probation, who comes to your aid? In many cases the problem is not that you are failing to execute your mission. Often the problem is that you lack the resources to employ the staff to gather the data, analyze the data, and present those data in an acceptable format to prove that you are executing your mission. The point is that being an effective institution and presenting documentation that an institution is effective are two separate things. I believe that higher education and the public would be better served if accrediting organizations which plan to take something from an institution by labeling it with warning or probation, or unaccredited should bear the burden of documenting that such an action is justified. And justification cannot be that the institution failed to provide the proof that it met the standards.

Dr. Hammer. I agree with your comments about accreditation. Keep in mind that there are people who are quite pleased with the current system and actually believe that it is working the way it should. The proof is that Stonewood is on probation. It is certainly true that we received favorable press. In next Sunday's paper a second article about the college will appear. The article will focus on why I came to Stonewood and it should contain several photographs. At first I thought of discouraging the reporter, but I decided that the positive press would help us with fundraising and ultimately with reaffirmation of accreditation.

I met with the President of the Eastern Georgia Community College System. We talked about his need for residential facilities and the fact that his board chair has told him the board cannot approve building such facilities within the next five years. He is interested in our vacant residential facilities. If we sold those dorms to EGCC, then EGCC would operate a bus service between our campus and its main downtown college. The students would have special ID cards and could use our dining hall and attend events on the campus on a pay as you go basis. We are still in a discussion phase and I plan to share this possibility with our board.

Dr. Tullson. That's great. In arriving at a price keep in mind that we need six million dollars. If we had four we could continue to pay down the arrearage we have with retirement.

Dr. Hammer. I don't know if we can get that much. Those dorms are in need of some major repairs and renovation.

Dr. Tullson. I know. Keep in mind that you are also selling the land. Perhaps a lease deal might work.

Dr. Hammer. We will explore the possibilities.

Mr. Bessel. Dr. Hammer it will take about 2.5 million dollars to restore those dorms. As directed by you, I met with EGCC's director of facilities and we toured each residential hall. Although extensive work is needed in two of the dorms, he saw great potential in the buildings and in what they could do for EGCC. I think that EGCC wants those buildings. I agree with Louis that you should get at least four million dollars. Does Mr. Stanmore know about our interest in selling the vacant dorms to EGCC?

Dr. Hammer. I realize that our potential buyer is already sold on the deal. We don't want to jeopardize it, and yes Mr. Stanmore knows about the potential sale of the land and buildings to EGCC.
Let's begin preparation for the board meeting. I shall discuss the financial challenges that we have, and I will inform the board of our recommendations. I will call on Tullson and Bessel for the proposed sale of buildings and land to the EGCC. I will call on Tullson for the potential settlement of our debt to the U. S. Department of Education and I will call on Zillamen and Lemon for the plan to recruit Hispanic students.

As the meeting continues the lights grow dim on the boardroom.

ACT II

Rejections and Festering

Narrator. The Sunday edition of *The Savannah Morning Times* contains the article on Dr. Hammer and Stonewood. The article is flattering and supportive of the college. The article contends that the region has been enriched by the presence of this progressive, forward thinking, and creative academic administrator. It even suggests that the local public schools and public higher education in Georgia could benefit from his experience and knowledge.

The scene is now the kitchen of the home of Trustee Rayson. The lights brighten on the kitchen of Trustee Rayson. Trustee Rayson calls the chairman after she finishes reading the article. Chairman Eagles can be heard but not seen.

Trustee Eagles. Hello.

Trustee Rayson. Hello Eagles. Did you see that article praising Hammer in the paper? It is way over the top. There is something wrong, very wrong. That paper never wrote anything positive about Foucault, and he is a great man, and he was a great president. I tell you that reporter, LaPortier, is infatuated with Hammer. I thought the first article was ridiculous, but this one is extreme in suggesting that only this man can solve the problems that we have created.

83

Trustee Eagles. Yes I read the article, and I was surprised about it. I don't recall that Dr. Hammer informed me that it was to appear in today's paper. I agree that the article praises him prematurely. He has not achieved anything for Stonewood. At this rate, the man will be able to run for governor and win in a landslide. If we wanted to remove him at some point in time, we would look ridiculous. And that may well be the point to these glowing articles – to limit our options in controlling Dr. Hammer.

Trustee Rayson. Yes, it is probably the work of the league.

Trustee Eagles. I am not certain. Ms. LaPortier may believe all that she has written.

Trustee Rayson. Do you think that she is involved with him?

Trustee Eagles. No, there is no evidence of that. I don't think that he ever visited Savannah prior to his interview for the position at Stonewood.

Trustee Rayson. Well, I asked Alexa Bastrap what she thought about Hammer and LaPortier. She told me that she did not trust Hammer and that LaPortier had been seen leaving Hammer's office at night on several occasions. She suspects that they are involved.

Trustee Eagles. Involved in what?

Trustee Rayson. In an affair.

Trustee Eagles. I don't believe that. Mrs. Bastrap is not a reliable source. She would distort and misrepresent to suit her purpose. I think that you should leave that subject alone and not participate in gossip. I know that Mrs. Bastrap is on our board, but we both know that she has a credibility problem. We cannot afford to allow likes and dislikes to get in the way of our work as board members.

Trustee Rayson. Fine, I will leave the affair thing alone. I do plan to let Hammer know that we cannot be caught off guard by these articles. He has an obligation to keep us informed.

Trustee Eagles. We can certainly have a conversation about communication with the president.

Trustee Rayson. Okay, well, I need to go. I'll see you at the meeting. Good-bye.

Trustee Eagles. Good-bye.

The light remains on Mrs. Rayson. She uses the phone to place another call.

Trustee Rayson. Hello Alexa, this is Marva.
Trustee Bastrap can be heard but not seen.

Trustee Bastrap. Hey, good to hear from you.

Trustee Rayson. I just talked with Sam Eagles about the article in the Sunday paper praising Hammer. I called to let you know that we think that you are right. There is something going on between Hammer and that reporter for the *Morning Times*.

Trustee Bastrap. If we were not involved in all this accreditation mess I would begin to talk to other board members about getting rid of this man. He is not one of us and I don't think that he even likes us.

Trustee Rayson. He wants to be the most prominent Black person in Savannah and we don't need to let that happen. He thinks that with the help of his girl friend and the league he can achieve great fame. I believe that he is just using our school to get a better position somewhere else. We have got to stick together to keep this man from destroying Stonewood. He likes to present information as if he is smarter than the trustees. He will learn otherwise.

Trustee Bastrap. I'm going to let the alumni know the real story on this guy. It will help them understand that the stories in the *Morning Times* are not objective.

Trustee Rayson. Well Alexa, I've got to run. But remember, we must stick together in this fight. Good-bye.

Trustee Bastrap. Good-bye.

The lights on Trustee Rayson grow dim
The scene is back at the boardroom. The lights brighten on the right imaginary wall of the boardroom.

Dean Bennings emerges from the wall.

Dean Bennings. It's difficult to understand how the college will survive. Some of these folk don't realize that they are the enemy. The college needs a loyal friend – someone whose dedication cannot be compromised. Now, Dr. Hammer is capable, but is rendered vulnerable by his misguided belief that in order to obtain the support of the business community he must please them and follow the advice of Jackson Stanmore. Chairman Eagles allows his ego to get in the way. He has used the college from time to time for his own narrow interest. You know that the land deal had to involve the leaders of the board in some way. Trustees Rayson and Bastrap are very dangerous. They would never allow the truth to influence their views. They openly profess loyalty to Stonewood, but they don't mind plotting to destroy Dr. Hammer. Now comes the board meeting. Dr Hammer and his team are optimistic and focused on restoring the accreditation of the college. Some of the trustees have as their focus limiting the rising influence of the president. What does the league really want? Is the league fearful that Dr. Hammer and his team might succeed? Is the role of Mr. Stanmore to ensure failure? The forces against Stonewood, direct and indirect, thoughtful and inept, will be difficult to overcome. Perhaps by grace, perhaps by grace.

The lights on Dean Bennings dim as he fades into the wall.

The lights slowly brighten on the boardroom.

Narrator. It is October 21. The fall meeting of the Stonewood Board of Trustees is in process. Doctors Zillamen and Lemon are completing their presentation on the plan to recruit Hispanic students. Dr. Zillamen is summarizing the report.

Dr. Zillamen. The recruitment of Hispanic students is a practical, prudent, and progressive strategy for stabilizing and growing the enrollment. It will build our relationship with America's fastest growing minority population. It will also make us more attractive to all potential applicants.

Dr. Hammer. Mr. Chairman and members of the board, I move acceptance of the report on the administration's plan to recruit Hispanic students.

Trustee Winter. Second.

Chair Eagles. It has been properly moved and seconded that we accept the report on the administration's plan to recruit Hispanic students. Are you ready for the question?

Trustee Rayson. Mr. Chairman, Mr. Chairman. Unreadiness.

Chair Eagles. Yes Mrs. Rayson. State your unreadiness.

Trustee Rayson. I just have a question. Does this mean that we are approving the plan?

Chair Eagles. No. The motion is to accept the report. Are you ready for the question? All in favor, please say Aye.

Aye!

Chair Eagles. Opposers, please say Nay.

Silence.

Chair Eagles. Dr. Melvins, please note in the minutes that there were eight votes in favor and three abstentions. The chair recognizes Dr. Hammer.

Dr. Hammer. As the board is aware, we are in engaged in a struggle to preserve the accreditation of the college. Financial stability is what we must demonstrate after a number of years of demonstrating instability. Enrollment has been in decline. We cannot argue that we can arrest that decline by doing the same things that have characterized our recruitment efforts. The plan to recruit Hispanic students will not change our history; nor will it change the character of the institution. The proposed recruitment program will enrich our environment and, significantly, yield for us an enrollment of 4,000 students in three years. This will occur in spite of the fact that we will continue to experience a decline in the African American enrollment. This plan is good for Stonewood. I move approval of the plan to recruit Hispanic students.

Trustee Melvins. Second.

Chair Eagles. Is there discussion of the motion?

Trustee Bastrap. I don't usually say a lot in these meetings, but today I must speak. I am opposed to this plan to recruit Hispanic students. Stonewood is a historically Black college. What would the alumni say about a board that would do this? This plan, if approved, will destroy the college as we know it. We expect the administration to bring us reasonable proposals and solutions. Instead, they bring us a plan that will ensure the destruction of our college.

Chair Eagles. Other questions or comments? Yes, Trustee Rayson.

Trustee Rayson. This motion must be rejected, if we care about this college. We know Stonewood, we attended Stonewood, we love our school, and we cannot let people who know nothing about it destroy it. There are Black students out there who will attend Stonewood. Why don't Dr. Hammer and his team present us a plan on how they will recruit these students? I cannot believe that this plan represents the best that we can do. I also cannot believe that the administration would show so little respect for this board. I am concerned about the direction of the college under the leadership of Dr. Hammer.

Trustee Winter. Mr. Chairman, point of order.

Chair Eagles. State your point.

Trustee Winter. Dr. Hammer is not the subject of the motion, nor is the administration.

Chair Eagles. Your point is accepted. Mrs. Rayson, your comments about the administration and Dr. Hammer are not germane to this discussion, and

Trustee Rayson interrupts the chair.

Trustee Rayson. I withdraw my last two comments.

Chair Eagles. Let us make certain that our remarks are to the subject under discussion. The chair recognizes Trustee Winter.

Trustee Winter. We need to recognize the position that Stonewood is in. This college could easily lose its accreditation. We are close to joining other institutions that have run afoul of the Atlantic Association. The plan may make some of us uncomfortable, but I am certain that we cannot survive operating the way we have operated in the past. If the plan will keep us moving forward, then I am for it.

Chair Eagles. The chair recognizes Trustee Melvins.

Trustee Melvins. I think we need to consider the proposal by President Hammer and his team. What are the alternatives? Time is a critical factor. We all know that opportunities have been lost and that we did not suddenly get in this position. We need to put emotion aside and focus on strategies that are likely to aid us in retaining accreditation and increasing the enrollment.

Chair Eagles. Reverend Raymondale.

Trustee Raymondale. We have been around a long time. In spite of the Atlantic Association we are not going out of business. I commend Dr. Hammer and the vice presidents for their work on this plan; however, I cannot support it. We need to remember who we are and why we exist, which means we need to remember our mission. I think the character of this college will be jeopardized if this plan is approved. I know the administration is under great pressure to ensure that we do not lose accreditation. I regret that Dr. Hammer has not given us something that we could all rally behind.

Chair Eagles. Thank you. Reverend Winter.

Trustee Winter. It is difficult for me to understand the opposition to the plan. Our situation is critical. We already have Hispanic students enrolled. We also have a few white students. Like many HBC's this is not new. The character of Stonewood has not changed. Now, Dr. Hammer understands that the future of the college is at risk, and he has presented a plan, which is grounded in the reality of American demographics.

Chair Eagles. I am not going to speak on this issue. Are there other comments or questions? (Trustee Rayson waves her right arm in the air and starts to rise.) Very well, Trustee Rayson.

Trustee Rayson. I wish to offer a substitution motion. I move that the plan to recruit Hispanic students be tabled until such time that the administration offers a plan to increase the enrollment of African American students.

Trustee Bastrap. I second that motion.

Chair Eagles. We have a substitute motion. It has been moved and seconded that the plan to recruit Hispanic students be tabled until such time that the administration presents a plan to increase the enrollment of African American students. Are you ready for the question?

Trustee Melvins. We don't have time to play games. The African American enrollment at Stonewood has been in decline for several years. You did hear in the presentation that the administration projects that the increase in Hispanic enrollment will lead to more African American students choosing Stonewood. Dr. Hammer could argue that he has already presented you with a plan to increase African American enrollment.

Chair Eagles. The chair recognizes Trustee Bastrap.

Trustee Bastrap. I wish to offer an amendment to the substitute motion. The amendment is that the requirement that the administration present a plan to increase the enrollment of African American students be dropped.

Trustee Rayson. The amendment is acceptable to me.

Chair Eagles. Without objection we shall now vote on the amended substitute motion. All in favor of tabling the plan to recruit Hispanic students please raise your right hand.
I count eight in favor of the motion to table the plan to recruit Hispanic students.

Opposers of the motion to table the plan, please raise your right hand. I count three. The plan is hereby tabled indefinitely. Dr. Hammer, do you understand?

Dr. Hammer. Yes I do.

Chair Eagles. Let's move to the next agenda item. Dr. Hammer.

Dr. Hammer. The next item is the college's debt for residential facilities that were built during the Foucault administration. As you know we have five residential halls that are vacant. The need for these dorms was never realized. The college has not consistently serviced this debt. Consequently, it has increased and as of the first of this month the amount owed was twenty million dollars. We have had discussions with senior staff members representing the Secretary of the U. S. Department of Education, and they are willing to accept ten cents per dollar owed. This means that we have the opportunity to resolve this issue for two million dollars. It is an opportunity that we cannot allow to pass.

The residential halls in question need a great deal of work. It would take over two million dollars to bring all five of them into operation. Fortunately they are somewhat isolated from the heart of the campus and are not seen by visitors. We have had discussions with the Eastern Georgia Community College System President about their openly expressed plan to obtain residential facilities. The president is interested in purchasing the dormitories and the land on which they sit. He has board support to pursue a deal with us. If we sell the dorms and land to EGCC, we can use the proceeds to address our long-standing debt with the Department of Education. EGCC will renovate the dorms and make improvements to land around the dorms. Sidewalks will be redone and the adjacent streets will be repaved. EGCC will provide bus service between Stonewood and its campuses. The EGCC students will be allowed to attend events at Stonewood provided they pay whatever we charge students. They will also be able to purchase meals in our dining hall. We think that these are good deals for the college. Dr. Tullson has prepared a presentation, which provides an analysis that is thorough and persuasive. It is found in your packets. I am certain that the Atlantic Association will find these deals prudent and wise, since they remove major barriers to the demonstration of financial stability. Therefore, we seek approval from the board to proceed with the sale of the dorms and the land to the EGCC for a price of at least two million dollars. We also seek approval of the board to proceed with paying the Department of Education two million dollars to settle our current debt of twenty million dollars.

Chair Eagles. Do we have questions or comments? Yes, Trustee Rayson.

Trustee Rayson. I realize that we have some major problems, but it seems to me that you only propose solutions that will drastically change the college. I cannot argue against the settlement with the Department of Education, but I am against selling our property. I don't like the idea of having those community college students on our campus. They will have no real connection to this community and its history. I can foresee them having problems with our students and staff.

Chair Eagles. Thank you. The chair recognizes Reverend Winter.

Reverend Winter. I want to congratulate the president and the vice presidents on providing us a way out of the hole that we placed ourselves in with some bad decisions. I am amazed at the creativity you and your team have displayed in a short period of time. I support the sale to EGCC and I strongly support the plan to eliminate the debt. If the board decides not to sell the land and buildings, then the board will have to raise the two million dollars. That will be a real challenge, but I believe that we can do it.

Chair Eagles. Trustee Bastrap.

Trustee Bastrap. I know that the alumni of this college are going to think that we have lost our minds if we sell off what Dr. Foucault worked and struggled to build.
I am against selling anything to EGCC. I believe the alumni would initiate a campaign to change the leadership of Stonewood. I am opposed to selling any of our assets.

Chair Eagles. Reverend Raymondale.

Reverend Raymondale. The proposal to sell a part of our campus is divisive. It may solve one problem, but it will create problems with our alumni, students, and many of our supporters. It could easily polarize our community and make other ventures difficult, if not impossible. Perhaps we should consider raising the two million dollars.

Chair Eagles. Thank you Reverend Raymondale. Trustee Melvins.

Trustee Melvins. I know that many of us may get emotional about parts of the campus and would like to see additions and never any subtractions. Many of the alumni and so-called supporters who would oppose the proposed sale have not given anything to Stonewood. We cannot base our decisions on who might be in opposition. We must act in the best interest of the college. The plans presented to us by President Hammer resolve some issues that I thought would lead to the closing of Stonewood. The plans give us hope; the plans give us an opportunity to recover, to grow. I encourage all of us to give the plans full consideration.

Chair Eagles. The presentation by Dr. Hammer requested that we grant approval to the administration to proceed to negotiate the sale of five buildings and surrounding land as described in the documents prepared by Dr. Tullson and to arrange to payoff the money owed to the federal government for 10 percent of the amount owed, which the government will accept as payment-in-full for the amount owed. Is that your motion Dr. Hammer?

Dr. Hammer. It is Mr. Chairman and I so move.

Chair Eagles. Is there a second?

Trustee Melvins. I second the motion.

Chair Eagles. Are you ready for the question? Because of the nature of the motion I am going to call for a voice vote. Those in favor will vote Yes and those who oppose the motion will vote No. Trustee Melvins, please poll the board.

Trustee Melvins. Yes Mr. Chairman.
 Trustee Avers. – "Yes"
 Trustee Bastrap – "No"
 Trustee Bellmede – "No"
 Trustee Blakemon – "Yes"
 Trustee Densley – "Yes"
 Trustee Melvins – "Yes"
 Trustee Pauls – "Yes"
 Trustee Raymondale – "No"
 Trustee Rayson – "No"
 Trustee Velcome – "Yes"
 Trustee Winter – "Yes"
 And for the record, Trustee Eagles – "No"
The results Mr. Chairman are that the motion passes. There were seven yes votes and five no votes.

Chair Eagles. Dr. Hammer you will keep this board informed about the progress on the negotiations for the sale of our property and the settlement of the debt with the federal government. I want to be clear on this. We do not want to read about it in the newspaper prior to being informed and the signing of the appropriate documents.

Dr. Hammer. I understand Mr. Chairman.

Chair Eagles. The next item on the agenda is IRS and Retirement Payments. Dr. Hammer.

Dr. Hammer. I am going to ask our Vice President for Financial Affairs to make this report. I am not aware that the board has ever been informed on this issue. We can find no record that it was ever discussed. Dr. Tullson.

Dr. Tullson. Thank you Dr. Hammer. Mr. Chairman and members of the board, Good Morning. Last month I was called to a meeting at the local IRS office. I was told that the college had been irregular following Dr. Foucault's indictment in sending the 941 taxes. As you know, these are the employee taxes withheld and the employer and employee social security and Medicare taxes. Although we have been making these payments since I have been at the college, we have a two-million dollar debt.

The IRS takes a payment and applies it to the oldest debt. We need to address this issue, since it is likely to be uncovered by the Atlantic Association. The local office of the IRS is not going to make this debt public, but there is a limit to the patience of the senior officer in charge. If this became known, it would make it more difficult for the president to raise money.

Chair Eagles. This comes as news to me. Are there questions? Yes, Trustee Bastrap.

Trustee Bastrap. Why is it that the IRS has not demanded this money?

Dr. Tullson. We can only surmise that the agency has been patient because in the two years that I have been here we have made payments timely. Apparently during Dr. Foucault's last year and during the next three years most of the quarterly payments were not submitted. We were surprised that the board did not inform the administration of this problem.

Trustee Bastrap. I can tell you I have never heard or read anything about an IRS problem.

Chair Eagles. It seems that the board was never informed about this matter. At this point, we should do our best to take care of this obligation.

Dr. Tullson. During the same period, we did not make retirement account payments timely. We owe about two million dollars.

Chair Eagles. Now, we did know about this problem. Is it not the case that these retirement payments are part of the ten million dollar deficit?

Dr. Tullson. Yes Mr. Chairman.

Chair Eagles. As we know, Dr. Hammer has proposed that we take the funds in the endowment to remove the deficit. If we do this the endowment will only have a few hundred thousand dollars left in it. I realize that the deficit is the next item on the agenda, but the retirement payments and the deficit are related so, without objection, I am going to ask that we discuss them together.   The chair recognizes Trustee Rayson.

Trustee Rayson. I am against spending endowment funds that way. I don't like it.

Trustee Bastrap. I agree. Somebody has got to protect what Dr. Foucault built. Dr. Hammer, are there other alternatives?

Dr. Hammer. Time is now a major constraint that limits the alternatives. Many of the companies that we owe are on the verge of filing law suites against the college. If this occurs, we will not be able to show financial stability. Additionally, some of the companies are now making it difficult for us to operate by demanding payment in advance. If AACS is informed of this, our situation is made more difficult. We have considered seeking a loan; however, our deficit, the money owed to the federal government, and the low credit standing we have with merchants in this city and region have led us to conclude that it would only expose how precarious our position is. When you combine these facts with the decline in enrollment that we have experienced since the end of the Foucault era you have a bleak picture. No first-rate institution will lend us money. Our struggle at this point is to resolve as many issues as possible, and to present to AACS a college with a projected future that is financially strong.

Chair Eagles. Very well. Yes, Trustee Rayson.

Trustee Rayson. Dr. Hammer, are you blaming us for these money problems?

Chair Eagles. Mrs. Rayson your question is out of order. Yes, Dr. Hammer.

Dr. Hammer. Trustees at this stage we have one interest, one goal and that is reaffirmation of accreditation. We need to pull together, to be together. We have no interest in blame unless it is the path to a solution for one of our many challenges. We are committed to informing the board about the state of the college. Apparently, we have found some historical events about which the board was not aware.

Chair Eagles. The chair recognizes Trustee Winter.

Trustee Winter. The best thing that this board has done in a long time was hiring of Dr. Jason Hammer. The effort made and the plans and proposals put forward give me hope.

Chair Eagles. Its rather late and I believe that we have covered the important agenda items. The remaining items are committee reports from academic affairs, and student affairs. Without objections, we will accept those as information.

Mr. Chairman, Mr. Chairman.

Chair Eagles. Yes Trustee Melvins.

Trustee Melvins. We have a report from the membership committee.

Chair Eagles. Yes, please make the report.

Trustee Melvins. The membership committee met yesterday and considered the recommendation received from President Hammer of Jackson Stanmore for board membership. Mr. Stanmore's family has been in this city for more than one hundred years. He is a highly regarded member of the business community and has built the most successful real estate business in Savannah. He is well known and knows his way around the influential and wealthy members of the community. We also reviewed his references and interviewed him. We believe that he will be an outstanding board member. Therefore, we highly recommend Mr. Jackson Stanmore for membership on the Stonewood College Board of Trustees. I move that Mr. Jackson Stanmore be approved as member of the Stonewood College Board of Trustees.

Chair Eagles. Is there a second?

Trustee Winter. I second the motion.

Chair Eagles. Are you ready for the question? All in favor please say Aye.

AYE.

Chair Eagles. Opposers please say Nay.

Nay.

The ayes have it and Mr. Stanmore is approved as a member of this board. Anything else Dr. Melvins?

Trustee Melvins. Mr. Stanmore is here. He has been waiting outside. May we invite him in to learn the results?

Chair Eagles. Of course.

Dr. Melvins goes to the office outside the boardroom and returns with Mr. Stanmore.

Chair Eagles. Welcome Mr. Stanmore and congratulations on being approved as a member of the Stonewood College Board of Trustees. Would you like to say something?

Trustee Stanmore. Yes Mr. Chairman. Members of the board I pledge to do my very best on behalf of Stonewood College. Thank you for allowing me to serve this great and historic institution. I look forward to working with you.

Chair Eagles. Thank you and again congratulations. If there are no other matters the chair will entertain a motion for adjournment.

Trustee Raymondale. I so move.

Chair Eagles. Without objection the board will stand adjourned until the next meeting in the third week of April.

The board members exit the room followed by Dr. Hammer and the vice presidents. Mrs. Rayson and Mrs. Bastrap linger and pause before leaving the room.

Mrs. Rayson. I don't understand Sam Eagles. He allowed all kind of nonsense to go on at that meeting. I had planned to go after Hammer on his affair with that newspaper reporter, but I let it go for now. Can you believe that we were the only board members who voted against having that plant from the league on our board?
If we are going to save this college we've got work to do.

Mrs. Bastrap. Well, I was also disappointed in our chair. I thought he realized that we have to stop this man. I am so sick of people saying to me how lucky we are to have him. That damn LaPortier has people believing that Hammer is the second coming. I am certain that the board will regret once again giving the league a seat on our board. I am going to let some of the active alumni know that we need to drive this man out of our college.

Mrs. Rayson. Well, let me get out of here, he may have the room bugged.

The last two trustee members exit the boardroom together. The light in the boardroom dims and goes dark.

Narrator. It is now early November and the college's administrators are at work.

The light comes up on Dr. Zillamen who is in his office. His phone rings and he answers.

Dr. Zillamen. Hello.

Mr. Eagles. Hello Dr. Zillamen, this is Samuel Eagles.

(Mr. Eagles can be heard but not seen by the audience.)

Dr. Zillamen. Good Morning Mr. Chairman. How can I help you?

Chair Eagles. I have been watching you and I think that you are a first class administrator. I am glad that you are at Stonewood. You know people call me all the time. I must say that the people who have called me have spoken highly of you. I think that you have a bright future at Stonewood and I wanted you to know that you have my confidence. If you need something, I want you to call me. After all we are on the same team.

Dr. Zillamen. Thank you sir. I am grateful for your confidence and your support. You are a legend in this community for your financial support of the college. I admire you and your many accomplishments.

Chair Eagles. Thanks. Now I need something from you. It is extremely important and it is a service that you can render.

Dr. Zillamen. Yes sir. Anything that I can do.

Chair Eagles. Good. Now this is confidential. I need to know that I can trust you. You know that I would make any sacrifice for Stonewood. I need to know that you are on the team.

Dr. Zillamen. I am sir. You can count on me.

Chair Eagles. It's Dr. Hammer. I need to know what he is doing. I need you to report to me what is going on at the college. As chair I need to be certain that I know the status of our operation. I want you to call me from your home phone at least once per week. I don't believe we can survive with the board in the dark about what could now take place between Dr. Hammer and Mr. Stanmore. I believe that we are in grave danger.

Dr. Zillamen. Sir, I cannot betray Dr. Hammer. I understand your concern and I am concerned about much that I see and hear, but I could not do such a thing to Dr. Hammer. I have never engaged in abusing and misusing the trust of my superior. I know that I said "anything," but this is a thing that would not allow me to respect myself and ultimately, I don't think that you would respect me. I am very sorry but I must say no.

Chair Eagles. You are making a mistake.

Dr. Zillamen. I realize that sir, but I just cannot do it.

Chair Eagles. You will regret your response.

Dr. Zillamen. Yes sir, I also realize that.

Chair Eagles. Good-bye.

As Dr. Zillamen attempts to say good-bye the phone line goes dead. He holds the phone away from his hear and stares at it before hanging up.

The lights go dim on Dr. Zillamen. The lights grow bright on the president's office.

Dr. Hammer is working in his office when Mrs. Wynn calls.

Mrs. Wynn. Dr Hammer, Dr. Zillamen is here to see you.

Dr. Hammer. Show him in.

Dr. Zillamen enters the president's office and sits down in the chair that is to the left side front of the president's desk.

Dr. Zillamen. Jason, I just had a conversation with the chairman that leads me to believe that we should all start looking for jobs. Because of the conversation, I know that I don't have a future here. Mr. Eagles called and asked me to report directly to him at least weekly on your actions. He thinks that because of the presence of Mr. Stanmore he needs to be informed about what you are doing and planning to do. When I told him that I could not do what he wanted, he told me that I had made a mistake and that I would regret my response to him. The conversation was very disturbing. Given my response, he knows that I am having this conversation with you.

Dr. Hammer. Stan, you have to understand that the old man is paranoid about white people. Although he may not trust my relationship with Jackson Stanmore, we must do our best to achieve reaffirmation. I think that in time the chairman will see that we are loyal to Stonewood and that he has no need to worry about the influence of Jackson Stanmore.

Dr. Zillamen. Don't you see that having such a conversation with me means that he has written you off, and because of my response he has also written me off. I think that if he could replace us tomorrow, he would.

Dr. Hammer. Stan we cannot do anything about the chairman's paranoia. We can only do our jobs. Our jobs are difficult enough; we cannot afford to gauge our actions and plans based on biases and attitudes of board members. Everything we do here will be judged critically.

Dr. Zillamen. I understand. By the way, in the meeting of the board committee on academic affairs Mrs. Bastrap opposed everything. We continuously informed her that we were only presenting information and not action items. Then she started to say that we were not doing a good job and to ask how what we were doing compared with one of the state universities. She was politely hostile.

Dr. Hammer. Don't worry about her. She will be the same at the next meeting. She does not present a problem that we can't handle. Be glad that you understand your opposition. I am going to have to end our discussion. Jackson Stanmore will be here in fifteen minutes.

Dr. Zillamen. Okay.

Dr. Zillamen leaves the president's office and meets Mr. Stanmore as he enters Mrs. Wynn's office. They greet each other with handshakes. Mrs. Wynn greets Mr. Stanmore and calls the president to inform him that Mr. Stanmore has arrived.

Mrs. Wynn. (Using the intercom) Dr. Hammer, Mr. Stanmore is here.

Dr. Hammer. Well, show him in.

Mr. Stanmore enters the president's office.

Dr. Hammer. Hello Jackson, good to see you. Take a seat.

Mr. Stanmore. Hello Jason, good to see you, too.

Dr. Hammer. One of the elements that will be in the report that we send AACS is documentation of support from the business community. Between now and July we need to raise money from local businesses. This is where I need your assistance. We want the businesses to give and to pledge annual support of the college.

Mr. Stanmore. I will prepare a list of businesses, which are likely to be supportive. I shall also list the CEO for each firm. I think that I can get the President of the League to send a letter before we make the ask.

Dr. Hammer. Time is not our friend. We would like to get these letters out before the end of the year.

Mr. Stanmore. Jason, we'll get it done. Now there is another matter that I need to discuss with you. Are you a candidate for President of Maine State University?

Dr. Hammer. Yes I am.

Mr. Stanmore. As I understand it you are a finalist?

Dr. Hammer. That's true.

Mr. Stanmore. Jason, how do you think the information about this is going to play?
Your staff and supporters are likely to feel betrayed and deserted. The business community is likely to conclude that you are dishonest, that you were never serious about seeing this thing through. The alumni who are under the influence of Mrs. Bastrap are likely to rejoice. Jason, you have a problem. If you don't get this job, you are going to have to work hard on maintaining the confidence of people.

Dr. Hammer. This is not something that I sought. A search firm that I have a relationship with contacted me and asked if I objected to my name being advanced, and I indicated that I had no objection. I did not expect to become a finalist. I thought the firm needed my materials to make certain that the pool of applicants was diverse.

Mr. Stanmore. That explanation plays well for how this got started; however, you would not be a finalist unless at some point you expressed an interest in having the process go forward.

Dr. Hammer. You are right. I guess with the almost daily discovery of another financial challenge and the built in opposition that we encounter from board members that I thought of a safety net in case this does not work.

Mr. Stanmore. I can understand that, but it is not something you can say to the public. I think that the business community will be sympathetic and give you a pass when I present what you have told me at the next meeting of the league.

Dr. Hammer. I am grateful. Do you think that I should withdraw?

Mr. Stanmore. No, I would play it out. If you are offered the job and turn it down, you will look like a truly committed leader, one who is willing to make sacrifices in order to save Stonewood. If you are offered the job and accept it, then you will be vilified. Some folk, however, will still give you a pass and blame some board members and the leadership of the alumni association.

Dr. Hammer. Suppose I stay in the search and work on my image problem and my efforts to preserve this college fail, what guarantees do I have that I will have a future in this city?

Mr. Stanmore. The business community does not want you to fail. You are well liked and you have shown abilities that many organizations would like to have their senior employees possess. You have not alienated anyone, unlike some of the local Black politicians.

Dr. Hammer. What about the ministers?

Mr. Stanmore. They will cooperate with the league. They always have cooperated.

Dr. Hammer. Even Reverend Raymondale?

Mr. Stanmore. Yes. Reverend Raymondale can be counted on to support what is good for business. He has big mortgages and needs to be able to count on the banks. I'll bet that you did not know that he was a part of the group of Black ministers who kept Martin Luther King, Jr. out of Dallas. He has been here about eight years and is stretched financially. He can be counted on to offset the local noise of the alumni association. Jason, cooperation is key for you to survive. I hope you understand that.

The light dims and goes dark on the president and Mr. Stanmore.

The light grows bright on Dean Bennings, who has stepped through the right wall of the boardroom.

Dean Bennings. It is difficult to have worked so hard to ensure that Stonewood would have a great future and watch as it sways in the winds of pettiness, envy, dishonesty, incompetence, bigotry, arbitrariness, selfishness, betrayal, authoritarianism, and ignorance. Now, some of what President Hammer wants to do is understandable. Because of the recent history of the college, he has been dealt a bad hand and his options are severely limited. I don't understand why he would run. But, considering the opposition from the board and the fact that the chairman has not embraced him, his exploration of other positions might be regarded as wise.
The league strives for control. You would think that the president knows this. His candidacy at Maine State University will forever be an issue. It could even be raised by AACS and it will, no doubt, be exploited by those who have decided that they want him gone. How will the end come? Will it be soon or will Dr. Hammer find a way to give the college more time? Will Dr. Hammer succumb to the lure of security and standing, which the league will offer?

It is clear that there are board members who do not believe in the institution? There are those on the board and certainly in the league who think our time has passed. AACS has sought vigorously to prove that the HBC's are relics of another era, using every opportunity to probe and investigate. Some have fallen, others are likely to fall. Some have mistakenly fought back with endorsements from high profile persons and a few have realized that the place to fight is in the courts. AACS will not admit to doing something wrong; that it sent a visiting committee to an HBC and not to a majority institution when both had been alleged to have violated the same standard. The fight to survive is far from easy, and Stonewood desperately needs some fighters.

The lights on Dean Bennings dim and grow dark.

The light now grows bright on the boardroom where the president is holding his weekly cabinet meeting. The president is speaking.

Dr. Hammer. I want to inform you that I am a finalist for President of Maine State University. You are likely to hear rumors and see newspaper articles. I did not initially seek this position. My name was put forward and I was asked if I objected to being considered. The search firm assisting in the search already had a file on me from previous searches. I surmised that the search firm was attempting to enrich the pool with some diversity and agreed to be considered. Well, it turned out that the committee liked by background and achievements. At that point, I could have withdrawn, but I confirmed that I wanted the position. Some persons in Savannah already know that I am a finalist. I realize that it creates problems for us and for the work that we are trying to do. It is likely that the search committee will send a representative to interview persons in this community about me. Some of you may be interviewed.

Dr. Zillamen. Dr. Hammer, some of the board members will use this against you and our plans to move forward. Some of the alumni will use it to solicit others to join their campaign to remove this administration. Even our supporters will now have doubt about your commitment. As I see it, we should ride it out and try to obtain some success that will offset the negative publicity.

Dr. Lemon. This is a major surprise. No matter what happens with the search, we are damaged. When the students hear about it the student leaders are likely to want to meet with you. Independent of how we got into this situation, you are going to have to declare your intentions. If you waiver, you will lose what standing you now enjoy.

Dr. Tullson. This changes everything. Some of us stayed this year because we believed in you. I don't know how I can keep many of our creditors from taking us to court. Many of my colleagues have told me to leave. They think that our situation is hopeless and that I am a fool for putting my family and myself in jeopardy. Just tell us what your intentions are.

Dr. Hammer. At this moment, I plan to stay. If that changes, I will inform you immediately.

Mr. Bessel: It seems to me that our credibility as a team is damaged. We need something dramatic to inform the public that we are still a team and that Dr. Hammer is still the leader.

Dr. Tullson. What do you want us to say to the people from Maine State University?

Dr. Hammer. Just be truthful and forthright. Address only the question that is asked.

The light dims on the meeting as it continues. The boardroom goes dark.

Narrator. The next day.

The light slowly rises on Dr. Hammer in his office. In walks Jackson Stanmore.

Mr. Stanmore. Good Morning Jason. I thought that I could catch you before you got started. I want to talk to you about Maine State University.

Dr. Hammer. Yes, a representative from the search committee, a Dr. Bentley Bankloo, is supposed to be on campus today.

Mr. Stanmore. Jason, you are not going to get the job. They have decided to go in a different direction and you are no longer the right person.

Dr. Hammer. But they are asking to talk to people in this community. It seems that the process has not come to an end.

Mr. Stanmore. If you mean that they have not announced the next president, then that's true. The next president will not be you.

Dr. Hammer. How can you know this?

Mr. Stanmore. I have made a living by knowing things before others did. It is a part of what I do. When you have information, you have options, you have power. Now you have the opportunity to call the search firm and the people at Maine State University and to withdraw. You schedule a press conference this afternoon on campus at which time you announce your decision to withdraw from the search at Maine State University. The work here was too compelling and you realized that you could not leave this job undone. You know the right words and the right spin to give it.

Seemingly dazed Dr Hammer mutters. Yes, Jackson, yes.

Mr. Stanmore. Good, let's get on it and call Ms. LaPortier and give her the information first. I've got to run. Use the information and use it while it has value.

Dr. Hammer. Okay and thanks. Thanks for everything.

Dr. Hammer sits without moving after Mr. Stanmore leaves. He stands and paces the floor as the light dims on his office.

The light now rises on Dean Bennings as he steps through the wall.

Dean Bennings. Dr. Hammer can't keep up with the game. He's trying to figure out if he is being played. He does not like his position, but his options were comprised sometime ago. He has to withdraw and exploit it to redeem himself in the Savannah community and with supporters of the college. I just wish he had a little savvy.

The light dims on Dean Bennings.

The light rises on Mrs. Rayson who is sitting at her kitchen talking on the phone with Chairman Eagles.
Chairman Eagles can be heard but not seen by the audience.

Trustee Rayson. Can you believe this nonsense? He must think that he can tell us anything. I knew that he is not committed to Stonewood. I knew that he was dishonest. I saw it from the beginning. I suppose now Winter and Melvins will see the true colors of this man. I'll bet that the league and their spy Stanmore were caught by surprise on Hammer's application for the job at Maine State University.
Now he wants us to believe that he is so given to Stonewood that he has withdrawn from the search.

114

Chair Eagles. I must say, I was very disappointed about his application for that job. I know we have not been as supportive as he may have wanted; however, I thought he was committed to seeing this thing through. I have been worried about having the league as a party to our deliberations and I thought that I needed to pay closer attention to what our president was doing and planning. I agree with you that the league was caught by surprise. I also agree that Hammer has probably lost some of the support he had on the board. What bothers me is that he is likely to look for other opportunities, and as much as you and Mrs. Bastrap dislike the man, he is the only horse we have in the race.

Trustee Rayson. I understand that. But just as he is likely to look for another opportunity, we ought to be thinking about who will take his place and what our strategy will be if we are faced with replacing him.

Chair Eagles. You make a good point Marva.

Trustee Rayson. I know it. You ought to listen to me! I know a little something about human nature. Did you watch the press conference? And why weren't you there.

Chair Eagles. I did watch the press conference. Dr. Hammer asked me to participate and I declined. I told him that I didn't feel comfortable joining him at a press conference on a matter that was all his creation, and that was damaging to the immediate objectives of the college.

Trustee Rayson. Well, good for you. Did you see that reporter, Jane LaPortier? In asking him whatever she did ask, she prefaced the question with so much praise that it made me sick. Aren't you convinced that she is involved with him?

Chair Eagles. I really don't know if they' re involved. For what is important to Stonewood, it doesn't matter.

Trustee Rayson. Oh, it matters. There are many white people in this town who would be upset with Hammer being involved with a white woman. They would want to see Stonewood fail.

Chair Eagles. I want you to be careful with that story. Don't talk about it. We are going to need Dr. Hammer to see us through reaffirmation. After that you can talk about it.

Trustee Rayson. I don't think that we need him. Given our history, AACS wouldn't dare take our accreditation. I think that we could find a recently retired college president with a distinguished record of achievement. Such a person could make us look good, while we find the right person for Stonewood. Hammer does not deserve anything, only to be fired at the earliest possible time.

Chair Eagles. I understand your views. We'll talk again soon. Good-bye.

Trustee Rayson. Bye.

Trustee Rayson immediately calls Trustee Bastrap. Trustee Bastrap can be heard but not seen.

Trustee Rayson. Hello, Alexa?

Trustee Bastrap. Yes, Marva. I saw the whole thing. Everything we thought is true. Hammer has been running the whole time. I knew he was coward. And Ms. Thing damn near confessed her love for him. I know the next time he talks down to us I'm going to let him have it. I think that it would have been good for us if he had gotten the job at Maine.

Trustee Rayson. I just finished talking to Sam and he knows that Hammer and LaPortier are involved, but he will not admit it. He thinks that we need this man to get reaffirmed by AACS. I am happy that everyone can now see Hammer for who he is. He keeps trying to make the board look incompetent with his discoveries. I believe that he's already in bed with the league, and Jackson Stanmore is there to make certain that Hammer only does what will make the league happy.

Trustee Bastrap. I know that we want him gone. I think if he goes, Stanmore will resign. Given all of our troubles at Stonewood, I don't understand why the league wants to keep up with what we are doing.

Trustee Rayson. I think it's left over behavior from another era. They are all control freaks. They think that if Black people do something in Savannah, they are not only supposed to know about it, they are supposed to direct it.

Trustee Bastrap. We know they've tried to control Stonewood since the Brown decision.

Trustee Rayson. You know, my son called the other night. During the conversation he told me that he thinks that the league is no longer interested in Stonewood. At one point they wanted to make certain that Black students had alternatives and would not seek admission to the University of Georgia. Well now that Black students are at Georgia they no longer see the need to support Stonewood. Their past investments in Stonewood were never about building a pluralistic society, only maintaining segregation. He thinks that they were happy when Foucault got in trouble because it provided them with a way to get off the board and to end the financial commitments that were made years ago. He thinks that they are worried that Hammer could succeed and they want to ensure that he does not, and that is Stanmore's real purpose.

Trustee Bastrap. Well, it seems to me he's got complete control of Hammer.

Trustee Rayson. How could a so-called smart Black man allow himself to be manipulated by people who obviously want us to fail?

Trustee Bastrap. I don't know, but I do know that you need to continue to work on Sam Eagles. I just don't see us making it with Hammer in charge.

Trustee Rayson. I agree. Let's stay on guard and focused.

Trustee Bastrap. Okay. Good-bye.

Trustee Rayson. Bye.

The lights dim on the kitchen of Trustee Rayson.

Narrator. It is now the third and final week of school before the December holiday break. Dr. Hammer has arranged to meet Ms. LaPortier in his office to discuss a third article that she wants to write about why he chose to stay at Stonewood. They are discussing the article.

The lights brighten on the president's office.

Ms. LaPortier. Dr. Hammer, what do you want communicated in this article?

Dr. Hammer. I want to convey to our supporters that I am here to restore Stonewood College and although I was being considered for the position at Maine State University, I did not actively pursue that job. I want them to know that my team is committed and that we strive every day with one goal in mind – reaffirmation of accreditation.

Ms. LaPortier. You must realize that what you are saying was revealed at the press conference and in the news reports about it. What is the theme for the article?

What is there to communicate that has not already been communicated? As I think about this, I don't see the value. It could come across that the *Morning Times* was being used as your public relations consultant, in which case we all lose credibility. Actually, it would be easier to write an article criticizing you.

Dr. Hammer. You are probably right. I have been so anxious to offset the negative publicity about the position at Maine State University.

Ms. LaPortier. I think we should wait until we have a news worthy event, which shows you as a great leader, and use it effectively.

Dr. Hammer. I agree. I will keep you posted on what we are doing.

Ms. LaPortier. Dr. Hammer, I would like to stay but I have some work that I must finish tonight. We can talk more at a later time.

Ms. LaPortier rises from her chair and moves toward the door. Dr. Hammer also rises and meets her at the door. Ms. LaPortier extends her hand and Dr. Hammer takes it.

Dr. Hammer. I am grateful for the support you have given me since my arrival at the college. I admire your work.

Ms. LaPortier. Thanks, and good evening.

Dr. Hammer. Good evening.

The lights grow dim on the president's office.

Narrator. During the December holiday break Dr. Hammer meets with Mr. Stanmore to review the list of businesspersons and corporate heads that Mr. Stanmore has prepared. These are the individuals from whom the college will solicit donations and pledges for annual giving. They meet on campus in Dr. Hammer's office. They are discussing the strategy.

The lights brighten on the president's office.

Dr. Hammer. Jackson I have reviewed the list you prepared. There are fifty individuals on the list and all of them have some history of being supportive of the college. Actually, their support began in the sixties and ended in the late seventies when Foucault ran into trouble.

Mr. Stanmore. Yes, and I am certain that they are prepared to once again support the college.

Dr. Hammer. Great. I have prepared the letters. The only thing missing is the amount that we solicit today and the amount that we ask them to pledge annually. The letter makes clear the importance of their participation and points out that they are contributing to our argument about financial stability that we will make to AACS next September.

Mr. Stanmore. Okay, let me see one of the letters.

The president hands Mr. Stanmore one of the letters and comments.

Dr. Hammer. The content is the same in all the letters.

Mr. Stanmore. This looks great.

Dr. Hammer. Now some of the individuals on the list once gave annually as much as $50,000. I thought we might base the individual ask on history and where there is no consistent pattern, ask for the maximum that the person has ever given.

Mr. Stanmore. We can't do that. We will not do that. We are going to ask for an amount that we are certain to receive and that these leaders will commit to giving on an annual basis.

Dr. Hammer. I don't understand why we would ask someone who has a history of giving to the college to give an amount, which is a small fraction of what he/she formerly gave.

Mr. Stanmore. Jason, you are overlooking some very important data. These folk have not given anything in the last six or seven years. Their motivation when they started gave Foucault leverage. You don't have that leverage. The colleges and universities in the state are integrated. And many of these businessmen openly question supporting Stonewood. They don't question the existence of the college. They don't even question the need. They do question why they should give to the college.

Dr. Hammer. It seems that the college's existence is more precarious than I had realized.

Mr. Stanmore. You can be successful, but it will not come in one fell swoop.

Dr. Hammer. So what amount do you think would be wise?

Mr. Stanmore. $5,000 now and $5,000 annually.

Dr. Hammer. That means $250,000 if everyone gives.

Mr. Stanmore. Oh, forget that. You will be doing good if you get 50 percent participation.

Dr. Hammer. My vice presidents are going to think that I have betrayed our cause by asking for a nominal amount from individuals who could easily give more. They are going to feel abandoned.

Mr. Stanmore. You are the leader. I am certain that you can control your team.

Dr. Hammer. Jackson, it is not a matter of control. It's about commitment and belief in a cause. They struggle each day with inadequate resources, trying to accomplish a goal, which many have already given up on. They believe in this place and that it still has great work to do. I understand your rationale for what we are going to do. I just want you to understand the consternation this will cause.

Mr. Stanmore. Jason, your options are limited. You need to keep the league on your team.

Dr. Hammer. Jackson, have you and members of the league had prior discussions about all of this?

Mr. Stanmore. No. I have not had discussions with anyone about my assisting you. I know, however, what these folk are going to find acceptable.

Dr. Hammer. Okay, let's make it work.

The light dims on Dr. Hammer and Mr. Stanmore as they continue to talk.

Narrator. It is now the first week of January and the president is meeting with his cabinet. Students have not returned and classes are scheduled to begin in two weeks.

The lights brighten on the boardroom where the cabinet meeting is taking place.

Dr. Hammer. In December I proceeded with the plan to solicit contributions from local businesses and corporations. I also requested a commitment to annual giving. I met with Mr. Stanmore prior to the holiday break and we got the letters out to persons he had identified as likely to be supportive. You need to know that we asked each leader for the same dollar donation and the same dollar pledge on an annual basis. That dollar amount is $5,000. I realize that you are surprised about the decision to ask persons who once gave five to ten times that amount to donate $5,000. Mr. Stanmore advised me that the amount requested was both practical and wise.

Dr. Zillamen. Excuse me Mr. President, I am not surprised, I am shocked and dismayed that we would aim so low, when our needs are so great. I admit, I don't understand it.

Dr. Tullson. Sir, I thought that we could get one million dollars from the community. Now, we're going to settle for a hundred thousand dollars. I know that you are committed to Jackson Stanmore and believe in him and the advice he gives you. I don't trust him and I believe that his role is to make certain that we don't succeed.

Dr. Hammer. Well, Louis, that's your opinion. I pressed Mr. Stanmore about the amount and he explained that no businessperson in this community has given anything to Stonewood in the last six or seven years. His argument, which I have accepted, is that we should build support in the business community.

Dr. Lemon. My concern is with AACS. Mr. Stanmore is not a consultant, but a member of the board. He cannot administer the college. If a certain amount of money is to be requested, then the full board should make that decision. If the matter has been delegated to the President of the College, then Mr. Stanmore has no role to play. He cannot use his relationship with you to guide you in directions that are contrary to board decisions or that take the place of board decisions.

Dr. Hammer. I understand all of that. When we send the report to AACS in September we must be able to show financial support for the college. We need the backing and commitment of the Savannah business community. Mr. Stanmore is the only viable path that I see for achieving that goal. I clearly understand the proper role for board members. You can be certain that if I reject the assistance and advice of Jackson Stanmore, then we will lose the support of the league.

Dr. Zillamen. It occurs to me that we do not now have the support of the league. Members of the league made a commitment to this college some years ago – it is a commitment that they abandoned when Dr. Foucault was indicted for misuse and embezzlement of federal funds. And I don't believe that they want to return to supporting Stonewood. I don't know what game Jackson Stanmore is playing, but he is not on our side.

Dr. Hammer. I do not believe that. Jackson Stanmore believes in what we are doing. Why else would he join the board of trustees? I am convinced that he is here to help us. He brings to us something we need – a way to gain the support of the business community. We will make all of this work. Now, let's move forward. Dr. Tullson where are we on the settlement with the U. S. Department of Education?

Dr. Tullson. Like you Mr. President, I worked during the holiday break. The Secretary has given approval to proceed. We can settle as soon as we have the money. In that regard Eastern Georgia Community College has also gained approval to purchase the residence halls and land on our campus for what their board termed a fair price. Sir, this gives us an opportunity to negotiate a price that will allow us to address the Department of Education, the IRS, and those retirement fund payments.

Dr. Hammer. Excellent, let's move with dispatch to complete the sale. I agree that we should maximize the sale price. You know that the board agreed that we use the endowment to take care of the deficit. Louis, please proceed with clearing those obligations that contributed to the deficit. If the sale goes our way we could have over two million dollars left in the endowment.

Dr. Tullson. I will.

The lights dim on the meeting as the cabinet members continue to talk.

Narrator. Later that day Dr. Hammer is in his office. He is on the phone with Trustee Stanmore. The lights brighten on Dr. Hammer's office.
(Trustee Stanmore can be heard but not seen by the audience.)

Dr. Hammer. We are ready to close on the sale with Eastern Georgia.

Mr. Stanmore. I know and this will greatly aid in repairing your image in the community.

Dr. Hammer. We are going to have the sales agreement drawn up tomorrow for six million dollars.

Mr. Stanmore. That figure won't work. The buildings are in need of serious renovation. There is plumbing work that needs to be done. Some parts of the buildings will have to be gutted and redone. And the folks at Eastern know that you desperately need to settle your debt with the federal government. They will not accept a contract for six million dollars.

Dr. Hammer. You know that we have other issues that must be addressed.

Mr. Stanmore. Yes I do and you should not make it public knowledge that you have an IRS problem and that you have been deficient in making retirement account payments. If that comes out it will make the institution look very bad and hurt you with fund raising.

Dr. Hammer. I don't understand. Have you and the members of the league decided on what successes we can have?

Mr. Stanmore. Absolutely not. You cannot manipulate the citizens of this community to pay for the bad past administration of Stonewood. You have community sympathy about the money you owe the Department of Education. You must tie the sale of the property to the Department of Education problem and only that.

Dr. Hammer. Suppose Eastern Georgia Community College is prepared to pay more?

Mr. Stanmore. The folks there will agree to two million dollars. If they agreed to pay more, I am certain that they would insist that you renovate those buildings and improve the landscape. You would not be left with the IRS and retirement monies.

Dr. Hammer.   This is very frustrating.   I don't see a way to win. The board of trustees has given me the authority to negotiate the best price that I can get.   There will be a lot of questions about the sale price and probably a lot of criticism.

Mr. Stanmore.   I think there will be a lot less than you think. Everything will work out.

Dr. Hammer. Okay, I'll talk to you later.

As he hangs up the phone, Dr. Hammer turns away from his desk and stares out the window as if he is searching for something.   The lights dim on him.

ACT III

Success and Plotting

The Stonewood College Chapel is packed.   Journalists and television camerapersons are present.
The chairman of the board, the president and several board members, including the Reverend Raymondale, are on the platform.   Chairman Eagles strides to the rostrum.

Chairman Eagles.   Ladies and gentlemen, students, faculty, staff, and supporters of Stonewood College, I give you the man of the hour – our esteemed President, Dr. Jason Hammer.

Dr. Hammer. Good Morning to all those who believe in Stonewood College and its noble mission. Today is a day for which we have worked and prayed. We have completed two significant transactions, which make for a stronger Stonewood College and a stronger Savannah community. A few days ago we sold to the Eastern Georgia Community College five residence halls and the land on which they are located. This land totaling 19.5 acres is a continuous strip of land located at the far south end of the campus. It is accessible without entering the main part of the campus since it is bounded by a public street to the south, by a campus street on the north and is adjacent to a campus entrance gate on the west. The residence halls will be renovated by Eastern Georgia Community College and used to house 1,250 students. These students will have access to campus events and food service for which they will pay the same fees as Stonewood students. Eastern will provide bus transportation for its students between Stonewood and its campuses. The proceeds from the sale were used to settle a debt that Stonewood had with the U. S. Department of Education. Given some other actions we have taken to pay off creditors, the college is now debt free.

Loud applause from the audience with shouts of "amen, amen, praise the Lord, amen, thank you Lord, amen amen.

Dr. Hammer continues. This is indeed a great day and we are grateful to have played a role in removing an obstacle that threatened the stability of the college. We rejoice and we thank God for this monumental milestone. I ask the Reverend Justin Raymondale to offer a prayer, after which I shall take questions from the audience.

Applause. Reverend Raymondale rises and moves toward the rostrum. As he approaches the rostrum the lights dim.

Later that afternoon Dr. Tullson visits Dr. Zillamen in his office. The light brightens on the two men who are in conversation.

Dr. Tullson. We need to look for jobs. I know that we have had this discussion before, but the way Jason handled the sale of the property to the community college leaves all of us no choice. We are doomed to failure. Did you hear him tell the people that we are debt free? Probably Stanmore told him to say that.

Dr. Zillamen. It seems that it does not matter what we recommend to Jason, he can only hear Jackson Stanmore. It's very frustrating.

Dr. Tullson. You should start to call your friends in Atlanta. Some of the board members are going to go after Jason as soon as the opportunity presents itself. They will never forgive us for selling that property and they will never forgive you for proposing that we should recruit Hispanic students.

Dr. Zillamen. I know. And right now we have a second board in the person of Stanmore. He overrules everyone. He is eclipsed only by the league. Sadly, Jason seems to believe that the league controls everything in Savannah. I think that it is an illusion. I think that they enjoy the fact that many people believe that they control everything. I told Jason that we should try to raise money only from persons, corporations, and foundations outside Savannah. Once it was a fact of life that leaders of HBC's had to go outside the South to raise money.

Dr. Tullson. But he will not listen to us. I believe that Lemon and Bessel are seriously looking for positions. Dr. Lemon told me that she is disgusted with how Jason has responded to Stanmore.

Dr. Zillamen. You are correct that the board will move against the president. They will also move against all of us. It does not matter that such an action will ensure the loss of accreditation. Most of the members of the board do not believe that AACS will take accreditation away from Stonewood. They disbelieve the information we give them. They think that Jason is only about self-promotion and that the college is stronger than we claim.

Dr. Tullson. I am going to speak to both Lemon and Bessel.

Dr. Zillamen. Good. Well I've got a committee meeting in fifteen minutes.

Dr. Tullson. Okay, I'll talk to you later.

As Dr. Tullson leaves the office the lights dim.

Narrator. The Sunday edition of *The* Savannah Morning Times contains a featured article by Jane LaPortier entitled: "How Dr. Jason Hammer Saved Stonewood."

The light brightens on Trustee Rayson who is in her kitchen, where she has just finished reading the article. She picks up the phone and calls Chairman Eagles.
Chairman Eagles can be heard but not seen by the audience.

Chairman Eagles. Hello.

Trustee Rayson. Hello Samuel, this is Marva. Have you read the Sunday paper?

Chairman Eagles. Yes, and I saw the article by Jane LaPortier.

Trustee Rayson. When are we going to bring an end to this foolishness? Hammer is not working for Stonewood. He is working to promote himself and to please the league. I sat through that program in the chapel with tears in my eyes. We have lost over 19 acres of the campus. Our enrollment did not increase this semester and I heard that Hammer sent out fundraising letters to local business leaders and he asked each person for $5,000. Does that make sense to you? Who decided on the amount? Does this man report to us or not?

Chairman Eagles. I hear your frustration. I realize that we need him to help us retain accreditation. I also realize that he is under the influence of Jackson Stanmore. I did not expect that the league would warm to him right away. The events are moving very fast and we must be guided by reason and not emotion.
We never discussed the dollar amount that would be solicited in the short-term fundraising effort. I thought he would seek our guidance before sending anything out. I had assumed that the request would be different for different companies.

Trustee Rayson. You see. He dismisses us. I'll bet Stanmore decided on the amount to be requested. Can Hammer be so easily led? Well, I propose that we restrict his authority.

Chairman Eagles. Any restriction at this point would create problems for the college. We have to continue to play this hand. We can and will watch everything.
I shall request bi-weekly reports from Dr. Hammer. I agree that we restrict his authority, but it should be done gradually. At this point we should act as if everything is the same.

Trustee Rayson. Samuel, I will do that, but at the April board meeting I intend to challenge his leadership of the college.

Chairman Eagles. That's fine. Just keep in mind that reaffirmation of accreditation is our goal. We need Dr. Hammer at least through the next year.

Trustee Rayson. What about his contract?

Chairman Eagles. His contract is for three years.

Trustee Rayson. Okay Samuel, I'll talk to you later. Good-bye.

Chairman Eagles. Good-bye.

Trustee Rayson now puts in a call to Trustee Bastrap. Trustee Bastrap can be heard but not seen by the audience.

Trustee Bastrap. Hello.

Trustee Rayson. Hello Alexa, this is Marva.

Trustee Bastrap. I was about to call you. I know you saw the paper and the article by his girl friend. The whole thing makes me sick. We chose a man who comes to town and becomes involved with some white woman half his age.

Trustee Rayson. I just spoke to Samuel and he is ready to get rid of this guy. I think that the only thing that slows him down is AACS and accreditation. I wish that we had more evidence about their affair.

Trustee Bastrap. Well, someone on campus saw LaPortier coming from his office late one evening. I don't think that he goes too many places except to events involving members of the league. We ought to hire an investigator and nail his ass.

Trustee Rayson. That's a good idea. We have to be discreet. We can't make the board look bad and we certainly can't compromise our seats on the board.

Trustee Bastrap. I'll get Walter, the alumni association vice president to get someone who is not connected with the college to hire a private detective. How will we pay for this?

Trustee Rayson. I'll pay for it. I hope that we have what we need by the April board meeting.

Trustee Bastrap. I am sure we will. I can't wait. You know Marva, when we get rid of Hammer I am going to propose that the board name you as interim president.

Trustee Rayson. I don't know about that. My background is in business.

Trustee Bastrap. Exactly. Someone with the ability to run a business is exactly what Stonewood needs. You are the best person for the job. Other schools have had presidents who did not have backgrounds in higher education. You may be the silver lining to Hammer's tenure as president.

Trustee Rayson. Thank you for your confidence in me. If the board wants me, I'll do my best. Now, let's not forget our plan to get evidence on Hammer and his woman.

Trustee Bastrap. Consider it done. As soon as I hang up with you, I'll call Walter.

Trustee Rayson. Great. I've got to run. Bye.

Trustee Bastrap. Bye.

Narrator. It is now mid March, about five weeks before the next meeting of the Stonewood Board of Trustees. Last week Ms. LaPortier wrote an article proposing Dr. Hammer as Savannah's citizen of the year. Trustee Rayson places a call from her kitchen phone to Trustee Bastrap. The lights brighten on the kitchen of Trustee Rayson.

Trustee Bastrap can be heard but not seen by the audience.

Trustee Bastrap. Hello.

Trustee Rayson. Hello Alexa, this is Marva. You realize that the board meeting is five weeks away, and, so far, we don't have any evidence of Hammer's romantic involvement with Jane LaPortier.

Trustee Bastrap. I know. I speak daily with Walter Shreve and he reports that the investigator does not have anything. They were seen talking at a league-sponsored luncheon. They were photographed leaving at the same time, but they got in separate cars and went in opposite directions.

Trustee Rayson. Is this detective an idiot? Everyone knows that Hammer is involved with the woman. I don't know when they meet or how they meet, but I know what I saw at that press conference. The woman was all goo-goo eyes and she spoke in such a romantic tone.

Trustee Bastrap. What do you propose that we do?

Trustee Rayson. Let's get them together in the same place and tell Walter to get word to that detective to photograph everything.

Trustee Bastrap. Okay, but how do we get them together? We only have a short period of time.

Trustee Rayson. I'll give a dinner party at my home for Dr. Foucault and invite Samuel and his wife, Hammer and his wife, LaPortier, you and your husband.

Trustee Bastrap. His wife? Do we want her to attend?

Trustee Rayson. No. She won't attend. She is still in New Haven. I don't think she wants to live in Savannah. Actually, this is another reason we should not have selected Hammer.

Trustee Bastrap. Well, let me know what you want me to do.

Trustee Rayson. You should communicate with Walter. Let Walter communicate with his contact who talks with the detective. Suggest that he be outside my house that evening because Hammer and LaPortier will attend an event there on that day. We'll do this in three weeks.

Trustee Bastrap. Will everyone be available?

Trustee Rayson. Dr. Foucault is available. He has not been acknowledged by this administration at any event. He has not even been invited to a college event. They have acted like he doesn't exist. Dr. Hammer will likely be in town since the board meeting will take place two weeks later and once he learns that it is for Dr. Foucault, he will be compelled to attend. LaPortier will definitely attend. It's an opportunity.

Trustee Bastrap. You have got it all figured out. Hammer is not going to know what hit him. Well, let me get in touch with Walter. I'll call you after I speak with him.

Trustee Rayson. Okay, good-bye.

Trustee Bastrap. Bye.

The lights dim on the kitchen of Trustee Rayson.

Narrator. The dinner party takes place. The next day Trustee Rayson calls Trustee Bastrap from her kitchen phone.

The lights brighten on the kitchen of Trustee Rayson.
Trustee Bastrap can be heard but not seen by the audience.

Trustee Bastrap. Hello.

Trustee Rayson. Hello Alexa, this Marva. We've got him now. Did you see them last night?

Trustee Bastrap. Yes. During cocktails Hammer spent most of the time talking to LaPortier.

Trustee Rayson. Right and when it was time for dinner she took his arm as they walked to the dining room. Did you notice that his hand was on her lower back as he helped her take her seat next to him?

Trustee Bastrap. I saw his hand and I saw that she was comfortable. For most of the evening they seemed to focus only on each other. And then they walked out together. It was smart of you to seat them next to each other.

Trustee Rayson. Well, have you gotten a report from Walter Shreve?

Trustee Bastrap. Not yet but I expect that we'll have the photographs to bring his time here to an end.

Trustee Rayson. Yes. Well, call me as soon as you have the report.

Trustee Bastrap. I will. Bye

Trustee Rayson. Bye.

Two hours later Trustee Bastrap calls Trustee Rayson. Only Trustee Rayson can be seen. Both women can be heard.

Trustee Rayson. Hello.

Trustee Bastrap. Hello Marva.

Trustee Rayson. Oh, Alexa, I was waiting for your call.

Trustee Bastrap. The news is not good.

Trustee Rayson. What do you mean?

Trustee Bastrap. The detective reported that he walked her to her car and after what he says was a brief embrace they left in separate cars. He followed her and she went straight to her condominium.

Trustee Rayson. What about Hammer?

Trustee Bastrap. The detective claims that Hammer did not go to LaPortier's place. The detective reports that he watched her place until she left the next morning.

Trustee Rayson. Don't you see? Hammer is too smart for this detective. LaPortier took the long way home, which gave Hammer time to get there. He was in the condo waiting for her and the next morning, he probably left after she did. I think that this detective is an idiot.

Trustee Bastrap. I agree that they are aware that they are being watched and that they are attempting to avoid being observed.

Trustee Rayson. Did the detective get a picture of them embracing?

Trustee Bastrap. Yes. According to Walter, we'll have the picture tomorrow.

Trustee Rayson. Well, at least we have that. I wish that we had taken a picture with Hammer's hand almost on her derriere.

Trustee Bastrap. Now we don't have enough to go after him. I guess that we just have to wait.

Trustee Rayson. Yes, but first we must fire that detective. I've already spent $1,000.
We'll use our usual contacts to monitor what is happening on campus. He's bound to slip up.

The lights grow dim on Trustee Rayson

The lights grow bright on the boardroom.

Narrator. The April board of trustees meeting is in progress. The vice presidents, Mrs. Wynn, and all trustees except Mr. Jackson Stanmore are present. Dr. Hammer has completed an update on accomplishments of the administration since the last meeting.

Chairman Eagles. Thank you Dr. Hammer for that impressive summary of accomplishments of the administration. Congratulations on resolving the issue we had with the U. S. Department of Education. Are there questions for Dr. Hammer?

Trustee Bastrap. When will those students from Eastern be on our campus?

Dr. Hammer. As I indicated the renovation work, which began in January, is scheduled to be completed on July 15. New furniture and furnishings will arrive between July 16 and August 1. Students will occupy the residence halls in late August. I believe the date is August 24. Dr. Tullson, is that correct?

Dr. Tullson. Yes sir.

Trustee Bastrap. I still can't get over the fact that we just gave away a part of Stonewood. Our campus will never be the same. Why didn't we lease the space to them?

Trustee Winter interrupts.

Trustee Winter. Mr. Chairman! Point of order. The sale to Eastern is not on the agenda.

Chairman Eagles. Your point of order is not accepted. Please respond Dr. Hammer.

Dr. Hammer. Leasing was not a viable option because we did not have the funds to invest in renovating those residence halls. Eastern has invested over two million dollars in the renovation work on those buildings.

Chairman Eagles. Thank you. The Chair recognizes Trustee Rayson.

Trustee Rayson. In your report you discussed the past due payments to the IRS. Why haven't you solved this problem or at least proposed a solution?

Dr. Hammer. In terms of developing the report for AACS we have given priority to those issues and problems that have been cited in formal communication. The IRS problem is not known by AACS. The IRS has attempted to work with us in addressing this problem. The IRS would not like for this problem to become public. Now, the college has made all IRS payroll payments on time since Dr. Tullson has been here. As I pointed out previously, the college went through a period during which payments were not made. Because we have been timely in making current payments, we have generated some goodwill. Additionally, the positive press, and the support from the league have encouraged other community members to be supportive of our effort to preserve Stonewood, even the IRS.

Trustee Rayson. Don't you think that by this time AACS knows about the IRS problem?

Dr. Hammer. No I don't think that the Atlantic Association is aware of the problem.
If the Association becomes aware, then we'll have to address it.

Trustee Rayson. What about the fact that a discussion of this issue is in our minutes?

Dr. Hammer. Board interference in the management of the college has not been an issue for Stonewood. I doubt that our minutes will be requested since we are attempting to show financial stability. Moreover, the financial challenges that are known to AACS will constitute the Association's primary focus.

Chairman Eagles. Dr. Hammer, what about the retirement fund payments that have not been made?

Dr. Hammer. AACS is aware that we owed approximately two million dollars in retirement fund payments. Those fund payments were a part of the deficit that we addressed in accord with the board's direction.

Chairman Eagles. Trustee Bastrap.

Trustee Bastrap. Well, your plan for the IRS is to do nothing. Is your plan on the retirement fund the same?

Dr. Hammer. You have not understood. The two million dollars for the retirement fund was paid. It was part of the ten million dollar deficit that we began the year with. We are behind in our contributions for this year. We should be able to catch up this summer now that we are operating two sessions of summer school rather than one. The accounts of persons who retire or who leave the college will be satisfied immediately. This has been taken into account in our planning. We shall also address the IRS. Starting September of next year we shall make payments to the IRS that should result in eliminating this matter in two years. We want to do it without fanfare or notoriety. Of course we shall continue to make current payroll tax payments to the IRS as we have been doing.

Chair Eagles. Trustee Rayson.

Trustee Rayson. Why would AACS accept this plan to address retirement fund payments that are still not made timely?

Dr. Hammer. We have researched the issue and we have found other institutions, which are accredited by AACS and which had to engage in similar catch-up payment plans.

Trustee Rayson. Does Ms. Jane LaPortier know about these plans to address our IRS and retirement fund problems?

Trustee Winter. What sense does that question make?

Dr. Hammer. I cannot account for what Ms. LaPortier knows about Stonewood. I am able to state that she has not received any information from me, or my vice presidents about our plans.

Trustee Rayson. Do you deny having an intimate relationship with Ms. LaPortier?

Trustee Melvins. Mr. Chairman, Mr. Chairman!

Chairman Eagles. The Chair recognizes Dr. Melvins.

Trustee Melvins. Mr. Chairman, I rise to make a point of order.

Chair Eagles. State your point of order.

Trustee Melvins. The relationship of the president with Ms. LaPortier is not the business of this board. It seems to me that my colleague is attempting to defame and discredit Dr. Hammer.

Chair Eagles. Your point is not well taken. The integrity and confidentiality of our plans are of concern to this board.

Dr. Hammer. I have not had and do not currently have an intimate relationship with Ms. LaPortier. She has been a friend to the college and presented it in a favorable light to the Savannah community. Mrs. Rayson, I thought that you and the Chairman recognized her as a friend, since you invited her to the dinner you hosted recently to honor Dr. Foucault. If there is something that you would like to raise concerning my deportment in office, please do it. I regard Ms. LaPortier as an accomplished journalist, who believes in the mission of the college and who believes that the events faced by Dr. Foucault toward the end of his tenure involved unethical and, perhaps, criminal behavior on the part of persons at HEW.

Trustee Rayson. Have you ever given her information about the college before it was released to or known by the public?

Trustee Winter. Mr. Chairman, I don't understand the point of this discussion. I think that my colleague has gone far afield with her line of questioning. We are not helping Stonewood. I urge you, Trustee Rayson and Trustee Bastrap to be careful.

Chair Eagles. Some actions that are not known to everyone make this line of questioning appropriate and relevant. Dr. Hammer will address the concerns and questions of the board of trustees.

Dr. Hammer. I did let Ms. LaPortier know that I had decided to withdraw from the search for a new President of Maine State University approximately four hours before the press conference at which I announced my decision.

Trustee Rayson. This reporter knows everything that we plan and attempt to accomplish.

Dr. Hammer. The articles written by Ms. LaPortier have focused on me and not on any of our plans to solve or resolve problems. Your allegation is not supported by evidence. I invite you to show evidence that Ms. LaPortier has information about our plans.

Trustee Melvins. Mr. Chairman, may I please be recognized?

Chair Eagles. Trustee Melvins.

Trustee Melvins. I have been listening and I must admit that I don't understand the questions that have been put to Dr. Hammer. They don't move us forward and they don't seem relevant.

Chairman Eagles. Trustee Winter.

Trustee Winter. You are correct Dr. Melvins. Actually what is going on here robs us of energy and depletes our spirit. I regret that we waste our time on such nonsense. I am sorry for those who see the need to hurt this man who came to us in our hour of need. I want Dr. Hammer to know that he has my support. I continue to believe that he is a blessing to this college. I call on the chairman to keep the discussion on a higher plane. I hope that this discussion will not appear in the minutes.

Chairman Eagles. The chair recognizes Trustee Bastrap.

Trustee Bastrap. What some of you don't understand is that this city is full of rumors that President Hammer is having an affair with Ms. LaPortier and that it is compromising his work as President of Stonewood College. Anything that interferes with the operation of this college is our business.

Chairman Eagles. Yes, Trustee Winter.

Trustee Winter. Rumors, however prevalent, don't necessarily equate to the truth. If the discussion has been motivated by rumors, then you should be ashamed. Let's suppose that Dr. Hammer is involved with Ms. LaPortier. I can find no evidence that the relationship has interfered with his job performance. Under difficult circumstances this man has forged a path toward success for this college. And Ms. LaPortier has written articles that have generated a community of support that we have not enjoyed in over ten years. We could not pay for the positive publicity she has given us with her articles about our president. Ladies and gentlemen, I hope that this discussion has not been motivated by jealousy. You do realize that you are placing the school that you claim to love at great risk. You do realize that only a unified effort can get us to our goal.

Chairman Eagles. Dr. Hammer.

Dr. Hammer. Mrs. Rayson, do you believe that I am involved with Ms. LaPortier?

Trustee Rayson. I heard the rumors, almost daily, since shortly after you arrived. I can't say that I believe that you are involved. I do know that the stories about the relationship are everywhere.

Trustee Winter rises in disgust and speaks before being recognized.

Trustee Winter. And only you and Mrs. Bastrap have heard these rumors. This is irrational. It is without foundation.

Chair Eagles. Ladies and gentlemen, please wait to be recognized by the chair before speaking. The chair recognizes Trustee Bastrap.

Trustee Bastrap. Well, I have heard people that I trust say Dr. Hammer is involved with this reporter. I have also seen a photograph of Dr. Hammer and Ms. LaPortier embracing.

Trustee Winter raises his hand and rises from his seat.

Chairman Eagles. Trustee Winter.

Trustee Winter. So what? I have embraced you and you know that we are not involved. What else do you have to offer?

Trustee Bastrap. I have seen things that I would rather not say.

Trustee Winter looks at Mrs. Bastrap in disgust.

Chairman Eagles. Dr. Hammer.

Dr. Hammer. I am disappointed that Trustees Rayson and Bastrap have seen fit to allege that I am involved romantically with Mrs. LaPortier. I am not romantically involved with any woman, except my wife. Perhaps the fact that she has remained in New Haven has contributed to these wild allegations. I hope that we will not revisit this issue. I would not want Ms. LaPortier to learn that the Trustees of Stonewood College engaged in a discussion about rumors of an intimate relationship between the two of us, and that I was interrogated about it. I thought that Mrs. Rayson regarded Ms. LaPortier as a friend of the college, since she invited her to a dinner at her home to honor Dr. Foucault.

Trustee Winter interrupts.

Trustee Winter. Mrs. Bastrap, Is that when you got your photograph?

At that moment Jackson Stanmore enters the boardroom. Dr. Hammer stops talking. Trustee Stanmore apologizes for the interruption and for his lateness.

Trustee Stanmore. Mr. Chairman, colleagues, please forgive the interruption and my lateness. I apologize, but a family emergency delayed me.

Chairman Eagles. Very well, please be seated. Dr. Hammer, had you finished?

Dr. Hammer. Yes, Mr. Chairman, I had finished.

Chair Eagles. Dr. Hammer this board has no choice but to be concerned about anything that interferes with the operation and standing of this college. I hope you understand that in questioning you about the allegations of an affair involving you and Ms. LaPortier that Trustee Rayson and Bastrap were simply fulfilling their responsibility as board members. We all strive to serve the best interests of the college. There is no jealousy on this board. I want that understand by all persons in this room.

Chair Eagles. The Chair recognizes Trustee Stanmore.

Trustee Stanmore. An affair between Dr. Hammer and Ms. LaPortier? That's absurd. Since last fall I have spent a great deal of time with Dr. Hammer, introducing him to our business leaders and some politicians. Almost every evening, we have been at an event. If any affair were going on I would have seen some evidence of it. The man does not have a personal life. All of his time is devoted to leading this college. If this allegation is in the Savannah community, it is only known by a few people. I have not heard it before today. If it is prevalent in the Black community, the one person who would have heard it is Trustee Raymondale.
Reverend Raymondale what have you heard about this allegation?

Trustee Raymondale. Absolutely nothing. The first time I heard it was at this meeting and I can say that I did not find it credible. Actually, I believe that the board owes Dr. Hammer an apology for interrogating him based on a rumor for which no one has any evidence. We have a long way to go and what has happened here does not help.

Chair Eagles. It does help because it gets it out of the way. I think that Dr. Hammer understands that. Reverend Winter.

Trustee Winter. Reverend Raymondale is correct. This board should apologize to Dr. Hammer.

Chair Eagles. Trustee Bastrap.

Trustee Bastrap. I know that you all are anxious to move on, but don't forget there is the photograph and the stories that Trustee Rayson has heard. The Chairman has not commented, but he may have heard the same stories.

Chair Eagles. People on this campus send me letters and notes daily. I have received the allegation from people other than persons in this room. Trustee Stanmore.

Trustee Stanmore. This is unbelievable. Forget the apology. This has been divisive enough. Let's move forward.

Chair Eagles. I agree. Dr. Hammer, what is the next item on the agenda?

As Dr. Hammer rises from his seat the lights dim on the board meeting. After a minute the lights rise on the kitchen of Trustee Rayson.

Narrator. Later that evening Trustee Rayson is in a phone conversation with Trustee Bastrap.

Trustee Bastrap is heard but not seen.

Trustee Rayson. Alexa, I thought that we had him. If it weren't for Reverend Winter and that Jackson Stanmore, we would have been able to lead the others to suspend Hammer.

Trustee Bastrap. What about Reverend Raymondale?

Trustee Rayson. Before Stanmore arrived he would have voted with us. He has so many mortgages that he does not dare go against the league. Stanmore knows the bankers who hold those mortgages. He's dangerous and we have to be careful of him.

Trustee Bastrap. Well, what's our next step?

Trustee Rayson. We cannot use that picture. Reverend Winter would immediately argue that we sought to set Hammer up. He would launch into a sermon and we would motivate that Stanmore to search our closets for skeletons.

Trustee Bastrap. You're right. But what do we do? We can't let this man continue to lead our school.

Trustee Rayson. We've got to be cool until Hammer sends in that report to the Atlantic Association. After that we should be able to generate support for his removal.

Trustee Bastrap. Well, I'll continue quietly to let alumni know that Hammer is not good for the future of Stonewood.

Trustee Rayson. Good. Let me tell you about something my daughter told me.

As the conversation continues the lights dim on Trustee Rayson.

After a moment the lights brighten on the boardroom.

Narrator. It is now August 1 and Dr. Hammer is meeting the cabinet in the boardroom.

Dr. Hammer. Our focus is to finish the report for AACS and to begin the fall semester. We are projecting a small increase in enrollment. It is not what we wanted but at least it is not a decrease. Dr. Tullson, tell us about the elements that will suggest that we are stable.

Dr. Tullson. The twenty-plus-million-dollar debt to the U. S. Department of Education has been paid. The ten million-dollar deficit has been removed.
The fundraising effort in the local business community brought in $135,000 and an annual pledge of that amount. These are the strong positives.

Dr. Hammer. What are the other positives?

Dr. Zillamen. The enrollment decline has ceased. We will have an increase of about 5 percent. This is extraordinary, since other HBC's that have had problems with AACS have experienced continuous enrollment declines. We also have two new state grants, and four new federal grants. The indirect costs generated amount to about $300,000 per year for five years. We have not had any success with the foundation community. The looming specter of AACS waiting to close the doors of Stonewood has scared the foundations away.

Dr. Tullson. Lastly, giving by alumni has increased, but it remains considerably below the level of ten years ago. In the last fiscal year, we received $425,000, which is more than twice as much as in the prior year. Now on the negative side our endowment stands at $492,531, because of the withdrawal of ten million dollars.

Dr. Hammer. Now we know from experience these folks at AACS could use this report as the basis for other questions about our operation. Be prepared to address any follow up questions. The report should be ready by August 21. I want to share a draft with Mr. Eagles. We also know that if we receive any decision from AACS other than reaffirmation of accreditation, we will be labeled as failures. Even a decision to move us from probation to the less severe status of warning will not be well received by the trustees and the alumni. No account will be given to the difficulties that we have encountered – board dysfunction, incomplete records, possible malfeasance, a web of conspiratorial acts at the federal level driven by a personal vendetta, a legacy of bad decisions, a financial morass, a negative public image, and the racism which permeates American institutions. I am proud of the effort that we have made. I don't think that it could have been done better.

Dr. Zillamen. We understand. I think that all of us have been motivated by your leadership to give our best effort. I am optimistic that we shall succeed.

As the discussion continues, the lights dim in the boardroom.

After two minutes the lights brighten on the boardroom.

Narrator. It is now October 19, 1985. Dr. Hammer has just completed a presentation on the fall enrollment to the trustees.

Chairman Eagles. Are there questions of Dr. Hammer concerning the fall enrollment report? Yes, Trustee Blakemon.

Trustee Blakemon. Dr. Hammer, what do you project the fall enrollment would have been had this board approved your plan to recruit Hispanic students?

Dr. Hammer. Above 10 percent.

Trustee Blakemon. Would this have helped us with AACS?

Dr. Hammer. Of course. It would have strengthened our argument about program viability. The increase in revenue would have aided our argument about financial stability.

Chairman Eagles. Yes, Trustee Rayson?

Trustee Rayson. Why couldn't you get above 10 percent with African American students?

Dr. Hammer. Our market analysis shows that the pool of African American students who fit the academic, social, and financial profile of the average Stonewood student is not growing in this state. We are actually beating our competitors by attracting more than our projected market share of these students. In spite of the negative publicity attendant to our probationary status with AACS, we have remained attractive to some students. Prior to my arrival we had experienced a continuous decline in enrollment. But even that decline was not as large as the decline other schools in our situation have experienced. Back to your question. The pool is not large enough to support a 10 percent increase.

Trustee Rayson. Mr. Chairman, may I continue?

Chairman Eagles. Yes, please do.

Trustee Rayson. I think that the numbers are there. This is just another shortcoming of your administration. I don't know how we can expect to succeed when our administration brings us unrealistic proposals and then seeks opportunities to lament the board's rejection of them.

Chairman Eagles. The Chair recognizes Trustee Winter.

152

Trustee Winter. I have not seen an unrealistic proposal from this administration. I have seen some creative and thoughtful proposals presented to deal with the difficult problems that this college has. I reject entirely the remarks of Trustee Rayson. Next she and Trustee Bastrap will attempt to show us the picture that they alluded to at the last meeting of the president and the reporter.

The Chairman interrupts Trustee Winter.

Chairman Eagles. Reverend Winter those remarks are out of order.

Trustee Winter. No they are not out of order. Whenever Trustee Rayson attempts to show the picture you are going to allow it. So, let's show it. Let's see the agenda of some of our trustees. Then we can move on to more substantive matters. Show the picture. Show it.

Chairman Eagles. Again sir, your remarks have nothing to do with the issue. Trustee Melvins.

Trustee Winter. My remarks are germane. Trustees Rayson's characterization of the proposals from the administration as unrealistic should have been ruled out of order. Her accusation that Dr. Hammer seeks opportunities to lament the decisions of this board should have been ruled out of order. And what occurred at the last meeting, when without justification, members of this board engaged in a witch-hunt, was absolutely out of order.

Chairman Eagles. Now you are attacking the chair.

Trustee Winter. I am not attacking you. I am saying that you have failed us and your responsibility to keep these meetings in the arena of issues that are our proper domain.

Chairman Eagles. The chair rejects the argument that it has failed to fulfill its responsibility.

Trustee Winter. You did not reject that nonsense the last time. So Trustee Bastrap, present your picture, characterize it and then allow the chair and Trustee Rayson to tell us what this proves so that we can move on. Show the picture, or admit that it is not relevant to our work. Show it. I dare you to show it.

Chairman Eagles. Trustee Bastrap, you don't have to show anything. Trustee Blakemom.

Trustee Blakemon. I agree with Reverend Winter. This matter needs to be put behind us, and such discussion should never again occupy the time of this board. What has been allowed in some of our meetings would cause us to be severely criticized and found in violation of some standard on board conduct. Trustee Bastrap, you should show the photograph that served to buttress the contentions made that our president had engaged in conduct that impaired his ability to do his job.

Chairman Eagles. Trustee Melvins.

Trustee Melvins. I also agree with Reverend Winter. We need to move forward. Trustee Bastrap you introduced to this board the existence of a photograph, which gave you pause concerning the conduct of Dr. Hammer. You should show the photograph. I also agree with Dr. Blakemon that we should not again revisit the issue of personal conduct without concrete evidence that the leadership of the college has been comprised.

Chairman Eagles. Trustee Raymondale.

Trustee Raymondale. I have worked with Trustees Rayson and Bastrap on many civic projects. I have served with them on this board for several years. They are exemplary citizens of Savannah. I doubt that they would smear or impugn the character of our president. I am certain that Mrs. Bastrap is not afraid to show the picture. I have not known her to be afraid of anything.

Trustee Bastrap jumps to her feet. Trustee Rayson shakes her head 'no,' but this does not stop Trustee Bastrap. As she reaches in her bag the chairman speaks.

Chairman Eagles. Trustee Bastrap, don't be goaded. You do not need to show anything.

At that moment Trustee Bastrap slams the photograph on the table.

Trustee Bastrap. Here is the damn picture. And you are right, I'm not afraid of anything.

The picture is passed from member to member and finally to Dr. Hammer.

Dr. Hammer. Mr. Chairman, may I speak.

Chairman Eagles. Yes.

Dr. Hammer. This photograph was taken in front of the home of Trustee Rayson. You can see it clearly in the background. I had attended a dinner to honor Dr. Foucault. You were in attendance along with Ms. LaPortier, and Trustee Bastrap. I had walked Ms. LaPortier to her car. There was a momentary embrace and then I went to my car and drove home. Was someone waiting to photograph me? At dinner, I was seated by the host next to Ms. LaPortier. I am dismayed by the implications of what may have contributed to the existence of this photograph.

Trustee Winter. And well you should be. This allegation of an affair never had any substance. Look at the embrace. Dr. Hammer actually looks uncomfortable. You could never construe the embrace as sensuous or romantic. Any contention along those lines is ludicrous.

Chairman Eagles. Yes, Trustee Rayson.

Trustee Rayson. I have acted in good faith on the information that came to me from multiple sources. I have no knowledge of the source of this photograph, and I have no knowledge of how it came to the attention of my colleague, Trustee Bastrap.

Trustee Bastrap. Mr. Chairman, may I speak?

Chairman Eagles. Yes.

Trustee Bastrap. The photograph was dropped at my home inside a large brown envelope. I do not know who took the picture. Nor do I know who dropped it at my house.

Ignoring the Chairman, Trustee Winter speaks.

Trustee Winter. Mrs. Bastrap, look at that photograph. How could you present to this body that you had a picture, which constituted proof that Dr. Hammer was involved with Ms. LaPortier?

Trustee Bastrap. It looks romantic to me. My impression was that Dr. Hammer was attempting to show affection discretely.

Chairman Eagles. The Chair recognizes Trustee Stanmore.

Trustee Stanmore. I know Ms. LaPortier and Dr. Hammer and I know that they have done nothing to deserve the allegations leveled at them by several members of this body. Trustee Rayson and Bastrap have made us libel to a lawsuit by Ms. LaPortier. The brazen zeal they have shown in pursuing this matter is unbelievable, showing total disregard for the college, and the individuals they have accused. I am convinced that this board should immediately go into executive session to address the misconduct of its members and the absolute lack of integrity in their presentations and representations to this board. I have evidence that they conspired to discredit Dr. Hammer, which I shall reveal in the executive session. In accord with our by-laws I move that the board of trustees immediately meet in executive session to consider the misconduct of several of its members, who have with malice sought to undermine and discredit President Jason Hammer and an outstanding member of the Savannah community, a highly regarded reporter for *The Savannah Morning Times*, Ms. Jane LaPortier.

Trustee Winter. I second that motion.

Chair Eagles. It has been moved and seconded that we go into executive session to consider the misconduct of unnamed members of this board.

Trustee Bastrap. The persons accused have not been named.

Chair Eagles. It is proper and consistent with our by-laws to protect the identity of the accused and to name them once we are in executive session.

Trustee Rayson speaks without being recognized.

Trustee Rayson. I want to make it clear that I have done nothing wrong. I have devoted my time and money to this college. It would be a travesty to accuse me of misconduct.

Trustee Blakemom. Mr. Chairman.

Chairman Eagles. Yes, Trustee Blakemon.

Trustee Blakemon. I move the previous question.

Chairman Eagles. The previous question has been called. All of those in favor please say, "Aye."

A resounding AYE echoes throughout the room.

Chairman Eagles. Those opposed please say "Nay."

Nay is heard from Trustees Bastrap and Rayson.

Chairman Eagles. Now for the motion to go into executive session. Those in favor please answer yes when your name is called and those who are opposed to the motion should answer no. Mr. Secretary, please call the roll and take the vote.

Trustee Melvins. Yes Mr. Chairman.

Trustee Melvins. Trustee Avers – "Yes."
                 Trustee Bastrap – "No."
                 Trustee Bellmede – "Yes."
                 Trustee Blakemon – "Yes."
                 Trustee Densley – "Yes."

Trustee Melvins – "Yes."
Trustee Pauls – "Yes."
Trustee Raymondale – "Yes."
Trustee Rayson – "No."
Trustee Stanmore – "Yes."
Trustee Velcome – "Yes."
Trustee Winter – "Yes."

Chairman Eagles. We shall take a ten-minute break and then convene in executive session. The administrative staff will wait in a separate area. Thank you.

The lights dim on the boardroom as the members walk out. Slowly, the board members return to the boardroom and take their seats. The lights on the boardroom remain dim as the members begin to debate – a debate that the audience cannot hear. The audience can see that Trustee Stanmore seems to be running the show. At that moment the lights brighten on Dean Bennings who emerges through the Boardroom wall to speak to the audience.

Dean Bennings. This is indeed a sad day in the history of the college. Lost energy, and a focus that does not make the college more viable. At a time when the college is vulnerable, we have people whose actions and plans are detrimental to its future. Their work argues that the college is now in a clime for which it was not intended. As Sara Teasdale wrote in The Long Hill:
I must have passed the crest a while ago
And now I am going down.
Strange to have crossed the crest and not to know
But the brambles were always catching the hem of my gown.

Can trustees who have a long history with the college be so petty and small-minded? At this stage the best interest of the college would be served by the removal of Bastrap, Rayson, and Eagles. The consequences of such an action would have to be addressed, but I think they could work it out with the help of Dr. Hammer. Well let's find out what the trustees have decided to do.

The lights fade on Dean Bennings who disappears in the wall. The lights brighten on the boardroom as the vice presidents and President Hammer return.

Chairman Eagles. Please come to order. The record will show that the board met in executive session and in that session the chairman of the board, and Trustees Bastrap and Rayson were charged with misconduct in the handling of allegations that President Jason Hammer was involved in an affair with a local journalist. As a result of evidence presented by Trustee Stanmore that Mrs. Bastrap was involved in the hiring of a private investigator to gather evidence proving the alleged affair, the board voted to separate Mrs. Alexa Bastrap from service on this board, effective immediately. Mrs. Bastrap, I want to thank you for your service to Stonewood College. According to our by-laws you have the right to appeal this decision within the next thirty days. If you appeal, a hearing will be scheduled within the next thirty days. If you do not appeal, or if you appeal and lose, the Stonewood College Alumni Association will be asked to replace you. At this time please gather your things and leave the meeting. Dr. Hammer, will you have someone assist Mrs. Bastrap?

Dr. Hammer. Yes, Mrs. Wynn will have someone escort her and provide whatever assistance she requires.

The Chairman continues his report.

Trustee Rayson was found to have shown poor judgment and admitted to having been duped by Trustee Bastrap. Trustee Bastrap confirmed that she misled Trustee Rayson. The board approved that a letter of reprimand will be placed in the file of Trustee Rayson. The letter of reprimand will be prepared by Trustees Melvins and Winter. It must be approved by two-thirds of the membership. The board exonerated the chairman of any wrongdoing. Now that we have taken care of that matter let's move forward. Dr. Hammer.

Dr. Hammer. Yesterday, we received a letter from AACS concerning the report we submitted early last month. The letter requests evidence that the college actually has financial support from the business community. We did not include the pledge letters because some CEO's did not send us the requested pledge letter. We have about 50 percent of the pledges documented and we do not anticipate any difficulty in obtaining documentation for the others.

Chairman Eagles. Is this the only request?

Dr. Hammer. Yes Mr. Chairman. The requested evidence is to be sent by November 21. We shall easily meet this request.

Chairman Eagles. I believe that you have a report on the athletic program.

Dr. Hammer. That's correct. Vice President Lemon will present the report.

As Dr. Lemon rises, the lights dim and go dark on the meeting.

After a minute lights brighten on the boardroom.

Narrator. Three weeks later, Dr. Hammer is in a cabinet meeting with the vice presidents.

Dr. Hammer. Our response to AACS is ready. I want to thank Dr. Tullson and Dr. Zillamen for their work in obtaining the documentation on the pledges. As you know, Mr. Stanmore was very helpful in getting the CEO's to cooperate. We shall send the response next week. Now, Dr. Zillamen, we have to appear before the AACS Committee on Accreditation Appeals to convince the committee that our accreditation should be reaffirmed. This will occur during the annual December meeting in Miami. Is anyone else here planning to attend the annual meeting?

Dr. Tullson. No, I need to be here.

Dr. Lemon. Yes, I'll definitely be there.

Mr. Bessel. No, I'll be on campus in December except for one week during the winter holiday break.

Dr. Hammer. Good, well let's get to work.

The lights dim as the vice presidents leave the boardroom.

Narrator. It is the second Monday in December and the meeting of the AACS Committee on Accreditation Appeals is in session. The case of Stonewood College has been called. Doctors Hammer and Zillamen have been introduced and are seated at the front of the room. The AACS staff representative for Stonewood is seated to the right front and to the immediate left of Dr. Hammer. He is Dr. Roland Saint-Amand, who has been with AACS for nine years and touts himself as the Association's foremost authority on historically Black institutions of higher education. His educational background is mediocre, except for an undistinguished period of service at a state college as a dean of social science. He takes pride in reciting the standards of AACS to whatever audience is compelled, out of respect, to listen. His constant self promotion and his way of finding a way to recite an accreditation standard in any conversation on any subject has caused some colleagues to label him as Monsieur Tartuffe.[1] In the past, Dr. Hammer has reminded his vice presidents to show all staff members of AACS respect and courtesy.

Dr. Jason Hammer and Dr. Zillamen have made opening statements about the stability of Stonewood College and the factors that point to its continued viability.

A committee member stands to ask a question.

Committee member. Why did you choose not to respond to the request from AACS about documentation of financial pledges from your business community to the college?

Dr. Hammer. Thank you for the question. We did respond to the request. We sent to AACS through Dr. Saint-Amand the documentation on the pledges made by members of our business community. It was sent via UPS.

---

[1] A comedy by Moliere about an individul who deceives his benefactor.

Committee Member. We do not have any such documentation.

At that moment Dr. Zillamen whispers to Dr. Hammer.

Dr. Zillamen. Mr. President something is very wrong. Why doesn't Saint-Amand say something? At that moment Dr. Saint-Amand speaks.

Dr. Saint-Amand. The committee has been provided with all materials received from Stonewood College.

Dr. Zillamen now feels compelled to speak. As Dr. Zillamen starts to speak Dr. Hammer whispers to him. "No."

Dr. Hammer. Mr. Chairman and members of the committee and Dr. Saint-Amand, I truly regret the confusion about this matter. Stonewood College enjoys a growing body of support from the Savannah business community. It is strong and vibrant. Some of our students have benefited from these relationships through internships and employment. Since my arrival, approximately eighteen months ago, we have worked to gain the confidence and financial support of the business community.
The League to Advance Savannah has endorsed and supported our local fundraising efforts. We have received donations and pledges from over 50 percent of the leading, well-established businesses in the greater Savannah area. The pledges are there and Stonewood is stronger today than at any time in the past ten years.

The chairman of the committee speaks.

Chairman of the committee. Thank you Dr. Hammer. You and Dr. Zillamen are dismissed.

As Dr. Hammer and Dr. Zillamen exit, Dr. Saint-Amand walks immediately behind as if he will pursue a conversation with them; however, once outside the room he quickly turns and goes in another direction. Doctors Hammer and Zillamen engage in conversation outside the meeting room.

Dr. Zillamen. Did you see that? Saint-Amand went in the other direction as if he is running from us. He knows that he received the documentation, and he knows that he failed to send it to the committee members. Has he fouled-up so many times that he could not own up to having mishandled our materials? Does he have any character? I thought he touted himself as the protector of the HBC's at AACS. We should sue. We have no choice but to challenge what happened in that room. We have worked hard and long to be reaffirmed. We have addressed major obstacles – obstacles that many folk work in higher education without ever experiencing. And now we encounter this backward-ass, characterless Negro, who represents himself as supportive and competent.

Dr. Hammer. You are right. I am disappointed in Dr. Saint-Amand. We will have to figure out our next step once we receive the final action from the Association.

Dr. Zillamen. Independent of the final action, we cannot allow our work to be misrepresented by AACS or anyone else. We must correct the record. We can prove when the materials were received by AACS and show that we complied with the request. You know very well that the people in that room doubted everything that you said. And when that Saint-Amand fellow claimed that the committee had been given everything that we sent, our fate was fixed.

Dr. Hammer. I know, but it may not turn out as badly as you think.

Dr. Zillamen. As badly as I think? Those committee members are convinced that we came in there with bravado and attempted to hustle them and obtain something that we do not deserve. We will be lucky to remain on probation.

Dr. Hammer. You know Stan I am very tired. I don't think there is anything else that we can do here today.

Dr. Zillamen. Okay, I'm going to go and have a drink. But remember we cannot rollover on this one. I hate to think about what Bastrap and her group will do with this. I'll talk with you later.

The two men leave in opposite directions. The lights dim. After a minute, the lights brighten on Doctors Hammer and Zillamen who are seated in a corner of the hotel lobby.

Narrator. It is now Wednesday afternoon. Dr. Hammer and Dr. Zillamen are in the lobby of the host hotel for the annual AACS meeting. They are discussing the actions taken by the Association at the business meeting this morning.

Dr. Hammer. Well Stan, they kept us on probation.

Dr. Zillamen. I know and we must sue AACS for violation of its own process and for dishonestly handling materials submitted. We have everything to gain. It's a no-brainer.

Dr. Hammer. I spoke with Stanmore and he thinks that we should go back to the drawing board and attempt to obtain reaffirmation next December. He's very thoughtful and strategic and I do trust his judgment.

Dr. Zillamen. This has nothing to do with his judgment. If we don't sue, we will confirm the committee's judgment that we are incompetent – that we have failed to fulfill our responsibilities as leaders of Stonewood College. Jason, the trustees have demonstrated that they will attack you without having a credible issue. What do you think this will give them if we fail to take on AACS?

Dr. Hammer. I am going to go back to campus today. We will talk more about this after the holidays. I am going to take off a couple of days next week. Exams start Monday and you should not have any problems.

Dr. Zillamen. Okay, will you be at home?

Dr. Hammer. No, I'm going hunting with Stanmore.

Dr. Zillamen. But Jason, you don't hunt.

Dr. Hammer. I know, but it will be a chance to relax.

Dr. Zillamen. I hope that you can do that. By the way, you should call Mr. Eagles. What has occurred here will be in the paper tomorrow.

Dr. Hammer. Right, I'll do that and I will send a letter to each board member explaining the action taken by AACS.

Dr. Zillamen. Well, I'm leaving. I'll see you on campus.

The lights grow dim as Dean Bennings emerges through a wall.

Dean Bennings. Dr. Zillamen has given the president good advice. Dr. Hammer seems to have more confidence in Jackson Stanmore's analytical skills than in his own. He also seems to believe that he will have another chance to obtain reaffirmation. It is difficult to understand how he could fail to hear his vice president for academic affairs. When I consider what occurred at this meeting I am reminded of a line from a poem that I learned in high school by Paul Lawrence Dunbar entitled: "Life's Tragedy." The line reads: "But deeper griefs than these beset the way."

As the light dims on Dean Bennings he utters: "Deeper griefs than these beset the way."

Narrator. The next morning.

The lights brighten on the kitchen of Trustee Rayson who is the phone with Mrs. Bastrap. She has the newspaper in front of her.

Mrs. Bastrap can be heard but not seen by the audience.

Trustee Rayson. Alexa, did you see the headlines?

Mrs. Bastrap. Yes. Stonewood fails, probation continues. It should have read: Hammer fails, Stonewood suffers.

Trustee Rayson. I had no idea that Hammer would give us the means to get rid of him. All you have to do is to be patient.

Mrs. Bastrap. Don't you think he'll have some explanation that will keep Reverend Winter, Dr. Melvins, and his other supporters in line?

Trustee Rayson. No doubt, he'll have some explanation, but if it involves challenging AACS, he will not be able to do it.

Mrs. Bastrap. Why not?

Trustee Rayson. Because he is controlled by Stanmore. After that last board meeting, I promised myself that I would take into account all the players in the game. Stanmore and the league would never want to support this Black school in a fight with an organization controlled by white men. The spectacle of such an event in a courtroom here or in Miami would be too much for the league. The members of the league would take such an event as a failure individually and collectively. Alexa you can be certain that Hammer will do nothing in the way of attacking or criticizing AACS.

Mrs. Bastrap. After all those fine words that Hammer gave us?

Trustee Rayson. Yes, but that was before Jackson Stanmore. The chairman is also very upset with Hammer and Stanmore. He blames them for the effort at the last meeting to find him guilty of misconduct. He will seize the opportunity to make Hammer's life at Stonewood difficult. The other piece to all this is that Reverend Winter does not like failure. With Hammer controlled by Stanmore, he will look grossly incompetent. That is not something that Reverend Winter will tolerate.
Hammer has no idea that this spring semester will likely be his waterloo.

Mrs. Bastrap. Will Stonewood survive this?

Trustee Rayson. Let's hope so.

Mrs. Bastrap. I can't stand the man, but what do you think could have helped him?

Trustee Rayson. He should have talked to Dr. Foucault. I don't think his ego would yield to reason and so he never did.

Mrs. Bastrap. Have you spoken to Samuel?

The lights grow dim on Trustee Rayson's kitchen as the conversation continues.

ACT IV

Waterloo

Narrator. It is now early January and President Hammer is meeting with his cabinet.

The lights grow bright on the boardroom.

Dr. Hammer. I don't want anyone to be depressed about what happened at the AACS meeting. We are still accredited and we have a chance, a good chance, to be reaffirmed this coming December. We will explain that AACS wanted more documentation and having another year gives us an opportunity to meet and exceed this requirement. I will make a statement at the faculty meeting next week. Dr. Lemon, I want you to make certain that our student leaders understand our status, and I want you to make absolutely certain that our recruiters and all admission staff members are able to explain that Stonewood College is accredited. It is important that all of you understand that I have decided that we shall not engage in any legal action against AACS. I don't think that our Association liaison, Dr. Saint-Amand, acted with malice toward the college. If we pursued this matter, Dr. Saint-Amand's tenure at AACS would likely end with prejudice. I am aware of some of his challenges, which I choose not to share. I know that we can succeed without seeking a remedy through the courts. I know that some of you disagree with that decision. I want you to know that I made it only after considerable thought and debating the pros and cons of the alternatives.

Dr. Zillamen. Mr. President, we have worked hard to restore Stonewood. The decision to keep us on probation conveys to others that we failed to do everything that we should have done. It gives our critics a weapon to use against us. Taking no action against AACS gives us no defense against those who will surely argue that we are incompetent and accuse us of all kinds of wrongdoings. Can you not see this?

Dr. Hammer. I see it. But this is a presidential decision. It is final. Does anyone else have anything to say on this matter?

Silence.

Dr. Hammer. Very well, let's move forward. Chairman Eagles, pursuant to the decision by AACS, has called a meeting of the Stonewood Board of Trustees for Thursday at 4:00 p. m. I do not want any of you to attend this meeting. You should be available in your respective offices while the meeting is in session. Mrs. Wynn will call you, if I need you. She will also let you know when the meeting has ended.
I don't want to see or hear any gloom and doom from the vice presidents. We will go about our work to build a stronger and better Stonewood College. Enrollment for next fall must increase; fundraising must increase; grants received must increase; and the scholarly output of the faculty must increase.

As President Hammer continues to talk about the work to be done the lights grow dim on the boardroom.

Narrator. It is now Thursday afternoon at 4:00 p. m. Chairman Eagles has called the meeting to order and Dr. Melvins has completed the roll call.

The lights grow bright on the boardroom.

Chairman Eagles. As you know from Dr. Hammer's letter and from newspaper articles, Stonewood College did not have its accreditation reaffirmed. The college was continued for another year on probation. As you also know, we had been assured by Dr. Hammer that the actions taken during the last year and a half would result in reaffirmation. Many of those actions caused consternation among the members of this board. Today we find ourselves still on probation and still in jeopardy of losing accreditation. We do not want for the meeting next December to lead again to another year of probation or something worse. So, Dr. Hammer please explain to us what was the basis for the decision made by AACS.

Dr. Hammer. The reaffirmation of accreditation of Stonewood College has been and remains the highest priority of the administration. We have addressed every issue and complied fully with all requests from AACS. Dr. Zillamen and I appeared before the AACS committee on appeals and made the case for reaffirmation of Stonewood. I thought that we made an excellent presentation. It was balanced, focused, and thoroughly addressed financial stability. In the end there were committee members who apparently felt that we had not offered enough evidence. So the recommendation from the committee was to continue us on probation. This recommendation was ratified by the general body at the business meeting. I have met with the vice presidents and we have doubled our resolve to obtain reaffirmation of accreditation next December.

Chairman Eagles. The chair recognizes Trustee Winter.

Trustee Winter. Dr. Hammer, I don't understand your statement. Specifically, what is it that we failed to do? What must we do differently this time?

Dr. Hammer. We failed to convince the committee that our financial base of support was strong enough. It was a judgment made by the committee.

Trustee Winter. Are you saying that the evidence was sufficient for the committee to have ruled or recommended in our favor?

Dr. Hammer. Yes I am.

Trustee Winter. Well, you have to challenge the recommendation of the committee as unjustified based on the evidence. Have you proceeded with that?

Dr. Hammer. We have not proceeded with challenging the recommendation of the committee. The only course of immediate action would be to sue AACS for violating its process.

Trustee Winter. Do you recommend taking legal action against AACS?

Dr. Hammer. No sir, I do not recommend such a course of action.

Trustee Winter. Why not? Please explain.

Dr. Hammer. We wanted to achieve reaffirmation, not through the courts or by some circuitous route. We wanted to achieve it with integrity – demonstrating respect for the process. We did not want to obtain it in any way other than following well-established procedures.

Trustee Winter. I know that you do not mean to say that issues resolved in court lack integrity. As a people much of our progress in this country has been won in the courts.

Dr. Hammer. No sir, that was not what I was attempting to say. It would have been better to say that we wanted to achieve reaffirmation the standard way.

Trustee Winter. Again Dr. Hammer I don't understand what you are saying. The situation we found ourselves in when you accepted the presidency was not standard. The standard way is meaningless. What should be our focus is victory. If you can't tell me how to achieve our goal, other than proceeding the same way we did before, then I am disappointed in you.

Chairman Eagles. Yes, Trustee Blakemon.

Trustee Blakemon. Dr. Hammer we want to understand why AACS chose to continue us on probation. You have offered to us that it was a judgment call by some individuals who found our documentation lacking. How do you prepare the next time if you were presented with something so nebulous as someone's judgment?

Dr. Hammer. We plan to maintain an active dialogue between the college and AACS throughout the year.

Trustee Blakemon. Your response gives me no confidence that we won't be in the same position this time next year.

Chairman Eagles. Trustee Raymondale.

Trustee Raymondale. Dr. Hammer, perhaps the objective is unobtainable. I was talking to some persons whose views I value, and they told me that they thought that the time for Stonewood had long since passed – that Stonewood belonged to an era that was gone. They argued that we are trying to preserve something, which is no longer viable. Perhaps the reason you can't offer more specificity is that the people on that committee see us as a dead institution.

Dr. Hammer. Sir, the objective is obtainable. Our mission is viable. Stonewood is valuable and is needed by this community, the state, region and the nation. An institution that begins with the premise that you belong – that you can achieve is and will remain viable.

Trustee Raymondale. So why did we fail to be reaffirmed?

Dr. Hammer. Trustee Raymondale we should have been reaffirmed. I regret that it did not happen.

Chairman Eagles. Dr. Hammer I am disturbed that you have no explanation for what occurred in Miami that you choose to share with the board about our failure to be reaffirmed. We have counted on you to be forthright with us. We have given support to proposals that you brought to us, although we may have had doubts. Now as the leader of this institution you come to this meeting with no more insight into what prevented us from being reaffirmed than the man in the street. Did we provide complete documentation on the pledges from the business community?

Dr. Hammer. Yes Mr. Chairman. We also shared that information with you.

Chairman Eagles. Dr. Hammer is there anything else that you can offer to explain the action taken by AACS?

Dr. Hammer. No Mr. Chairman.

Chairman Eagles. Yes, Trustee Rayson.

Trustee Rayson. I cannot believe that we are willing to accept what has been presented by Dr. Hammer. I suggest that we make an inquiry of AACS without use of prejudicial language about events and/or factors that contributed to the decision to continue Stonewood College on probation.

Chairman Eagles. Trustee Stanmore.

Trustee Stanmore. I think that we need to put this matter behind us. Any inquiry is going to raise other issues about the relationship between the board and the administration. Dr. Hammer and his team made a great effort and for some reason AACS decided to keep the college on probation. The president has recommended that we move forward and not allow this setback to derail the momentum we have gained. I know that some former major donors are planning to again provide financial support to Stonewood. These individuals have high regard for Dr. Hammer and the accomplishments of his administration. Pursuing this inquiry will scare some potential donors away. People want to be associated with success and not controversy. I also know that the league thinks that it could have been more helpful to Dr. Hammer. The thinking of the league's leadership is that reaffirmation of accreditation should have been granted, and that AACS made a mistake, which will be corrected in December. Thus, I strongly urge you to accept Dr. Hammer's approach and to move forward without making an inquiry.

Chairman Eagles. Trustee Winter.

Trustee Winter. Mr. Stanmore, if Dr. Hammer had provided something of substance, then I would agree with you. I am sensitive about the issue of unity and I believe that we should work harder to achieve unity on this board. I found the veiled threat about donors insulting. We have an obligation to protect the college and so Mr. Stanmore we must reject the recommendation made by Dr. Hammer and persuasively supported by you.

Chairman Eagles. Is there anyone who agrees with Trustee Stanmore?

Silence.

Chairman Eagles. Very well, we shall proceed with an inquiry about events and/or factors that contributed to the decision to maintain Stonewood College on probation
Without objection, I want Trustees Blakemon, Melvins, and Winter to proceed with the inquiry. I would like to meet with them at the end of this meeting.

Chairman Eagles. May I have a motion for adjournment?

The lights dim on the boardroom as the members depart. Trustees Winter, Melvins, and Blakemon remain with Chairman Eagles.

Narrator. It is now February 15 and Chairman Eagles has called another meeting of the Stonewood Board of Trustees. All members are present.

The lights brighten on the boardroom as Chairman Eagles addresses the members.

Chairman Eagles. We are assembled to receive the report from our ad hoc subcommittee, consisting of Dr. Blakemon, Dr. Melvins, and Reverend Winter, which was charged with making an inquiry about why Stonewood College was continued on probation for another year. Reverend Winter.

Reverend Winter. Mr. Chairman we followed the directive of the board and sought information about factors and/or events that contributed to the recommendation of the committee that received our appeal to recommend that we remain on probation.

We were led to make this inquiry because of the lack of specificity in President Hammer's report to the board. We visited the office of the Atlantic Association in Miami, Florida and met with Dr. Roland Saint-Amand. We had requested a meeting with the President, Dr. Ralph Bacone, but we were referred to Dr. Saint-Amand. We met with him one week ago today. He appeared open and candid and claimed to be a supporter of Stonewood College. When we asked for the specific reason the committee recommended a continuation of probation he stated, and I quote: "The college failed to submit timely evidence of financial pledges made by members of the Savannah business community." We pressed Dr. Saint-Amand for more information. He explained that his office prepared packets for each committee member consisting of the materials requested by AACS and the materials submitted by the institution. He told us that the committee members were disturbed that the college had failed to fulfill its obligation. He added that Dr. Hammer had maintained at the meeting that he had submitted the requested items on time. Dr. Blakemon asked if it were possible that AACS and the college had both acted in good faith. When Dr. Saint-Amand inquired as to what she meant, Dr. Blakemon explained that there could have been confusion about the date that materials were due. He then pulled a copy of the letter that had been sent to Dr. Hammer requesting the documentation on the pledges by November 21. Dr. Saint-Amand recognized immediately that the letter sent had a typographical error, the 21st should have been the 12th. On the 13th of November his office distributed materials to the committee members without having received the submission from Stonewood. Apparently our submission arrived on the 15th several days before the deadline that Dr. Hammer was using, but late according to the deadline that AACS used. Given that AACS had responsibility for the communication sent to Dr. Hammer with the wrong date, we pressed Dr. Saint-Amand about some dispensation for Stonewood College. He took the position that all ratified actions are final. In fact, he shifted the blame for the miscommunication to the college by contending that had the leadership at Stonewood been in close communication with him the typo would not have mattered. We found his position ridiculous. We also asked him why he did not distribute the Stonewood materials to the committee members indicating that they were received late. Then he talked about integrity of the process and treating all institutions the same. When we informed him that we thought that Stonewood College was being treated unfairly, he became argumentative and arrogantly told us of how hard he works to assist Black institutions. We were shocked at his lack of integrity. These are our findings, which we respectfully submit for your consideration and possible action.

Chairman Eagles. So, even in the face of evidence that the college suffered a negative decision because of his error, Dr. Saint-Amand was not contrite and offered no apology.

Trustee Winter. Yes. You would think that in his position that honesty would far out weigh saving face. The importance of making corrections is not on the agenda of Dr. Saint-Amand. It would seem that all decisions by such an agency would require another level of review. The job that the people at AACS attempt to perform is about a lot more than remembering and reciting standards, or probing our files and reading our meeting minutes. It would seem to me that AACS and the other regional accrediting agencies would have to adhere to a code of conduct about how they interact with the member institutions. The error made by Dr. Saint-Amand is understandable. The fact that he does not accept any responsibility for righting the wrong should result in him being fired with prejudice.

Trustee Blakemon. Reverend Winter has stated very well our experience, our findings, and our perspective. We were disappointed in the cavalier attitude of Dr. Saint-Amand. He literally informed us that we should be grateful that we are still accredited. And what was most disgusting was his subliminal message that we did not want to take on a fight with AACS.

179

Chairman Eagles. Are there questions for the subcommittee members?

Chairman Eagles. Trustee Rayson.

Trustee Rayson. What action do you recommend on the part of the board?

Trustee Winter. We did not formulate a recommendation. We thought that the full board should make the decision on how to proceed.

Trustee Rayson. I recommend that we sue AACS. The well being of Stonewood has been jeopardized. We have been treated unfairly and dishonestly.

Dr. Hammer. Mr. Chairman, Mr. Chairman…

Chairman Eagles. Dr. Hammer we are not prepared to hear from you at this time!

Trustee Rayson. As I was saying, we owe it to our students, faculty, staff, alumni, and supporters to beat these people in the courts. I realize that it could get expensive, but the pursuit of any other alternative would leave me feeling like a failure.

Chairman Eagles. Trustee Raymondale.

Trustee Raymondale. I understand that we are incensed, but our backs are not against the wall. We don't have to sue. Are we better off in dealing with AACS if we sue and lose? I think there is a lot more at stake than our bruised egos. At this moment I urge caution.

Chairman Eagles. Trustee Melvins.

Trustee Melvins. I am angry at the position taken by Dr. Saint-Amand and I am angry at the blatant dishonesty of Dr. Hammer. When we left Miami, I was certain that we had to sue and seek reaffirmation of accreditation as a remedy imposed by the courts. Today I have some doubt as to whether that is the most prudent course to follow. Putting aside his bravado, Dr. Saint-Amand is clearly comprised. He knows that this community is aware of his dishonesty and incompetence. It may serve our cause more to hold our current position and give him the opportunity to make certain that we are successful in December.

Trustee Rayson. Dr. Saint-Amand has proven that he cannot be counted on to stay with any course. He can be comprised by his desire to look like he knows what he is doing. Any expectation about his behavior is folly.

Chairman Eagles. Trustee Blakemon.

Trustee Blakemon. I agree with Trustee Rayson, but I don't think that we should sue. If we sue and lose, we will be in a weakened position going forward. Although Dr. Hammer has accomplished a great deal, we are far from being a strong institution. All vendors now demand payment upfront, we have no reserves, and we face challenges with the IRS that AACS does not know about. I recommend that we proceed with caution since there is no guarantee on how many of our problems may be exposed if we engage in a fight with AACS.

Chairman Eagles. I am disturbed by the treatment we have received and I would like very much to expose AACS in the courts; however, I share the reservations expressed by Trustee Blakemon. Unless there is an argument to support a lawsuit that we have not heard, I suggest that we take no action at this time. Trustee Rayson.

Trustee Rayson. I would remind the board that not suing is an action consistent with the position taken by persons whose loyalty is now in question.

Chairman Eagles. Trustee Rayson, we may very well return to your position. Now, Dr. Hammer please explain to the board why you were less than forthright in your report of what occurred at the AACS meeting last December.

Dr. Hammer. I presented to this body the information that I thought would allow us to move forward. I did not discuss the disagreement that we had with the committee and Dr. Saint-Amand about the submission of evidence on pledges from the business community. I did not believe that pursuing the disagreement was in our best interest.

Chairman Eagles. Trustee Winter.

Trustee Winter. Dr. Hammer what you did and just said don't make sense. You have nothing to gain by being dishonest. There must be a missing piece to this story. If you can't provide something more substantial than what you just said, then I don't need to hear anything else.

Chairman Eagles. Trustee Stanmore.

Trustee Stanmore. I think we need to hear President Hammer. He has experience dealing with accrediting agencies. When he and Dr. Zillamen appeared before the AACS appeals committee and engaged in a disagreement about the submission of requested documentation, Dr. Hammer made a decision that he would not put the college at greater risk by debating with the committee and AACS. He obviously made the decision based on his experience that the best course was to do nothing. He did not tell us everything that occurred. I have no problem with that. In fact, because of everything that has occurred, including the visit by Reverend Winter and his committee to Miami, we will be easily reaffirmed in December. I see no reason to berate Dr. Hammer. We do not need to be divisive; we need to pull together.

Chairman Eagles. Trustee Rayson.

Trustee Rayson. However you spin it, Dr. Hammer lied to this board and when pressed for the truth, he lied again. What are we going to do? That's the only relevant question.

Chairman Eagles. Trustee Raymondale.

Trustee Raymondale. Dr. Hammer you have made a bad situation worse. I have had doubts about the extraordinary efforts we were making to save Stonewood. I have pondered and discussed with others whether Stonewood is still needed. You realize that some of our former major donors have left us because they don't see the need for us to exist. Dr. Hammer, you caused me to believe again in Stonewood and now I find that you don't really believe in this college. If you were truly committed to Stonewood, you could not have done what you did in Miami, and then play a game with this board based on the notion that your thinking is superior to ours. I resent the betrayal. It is something that will be difficult to forget.

Chairman Eagles. Trustee Rayson.

Trustee Rayson. I move that the Board of Trustees of Stonewood College suspend with pay Dr. Jason Hammer from his position as President of Stonewood College effective this fifteenth day of February 1986 at 7:00 p. m. Eastern Standard Time.

Trustee Raymondale. Second

Trustee Stanmore. Mr. Chairman!

Chairman Eagles. Hold on. There is a motion on the floor. It has been moved and seconded that the board suspend with pay Dr. Jason Hammer as President of Stonewood College effective today at 7:00 p. m. Are you ready for the question?

Trustee Stanmore. Unreadiness.

Chairman Eagles. State your unreadiness.

Trustee Stanmore. An action this severe deserves considerable discussion and debate. Have we thought through the consequences of such an action? What will be the damage to the college locally and nationally? How will AACS respond? We could very well make ourselves the object of an inquiry from AACS. Although some of you may want to punish Dr. Hammer and to hold him up for public ridicule, we may encounter ridicule ourselves. I urge us to proceed with caution.

Chairman Eagles. Your point is well made. Is there further discussion? Yes, Trustee Rayson.

Trustee Rayson. You just want to save him. You don't care about Stonewood.

Chairman Eagles. Trustee Rayson your comments are completely out of line and will be disregarded. The Chair recognizes Trustee Winter.

Trustee Winter. We don't want to compound our problem. And we don't need to do anything that will damage our chances for reaffirmation of accreditation next December. I think suspending the president will lead to many difficult problems. I think those pledges from the business community will be withdrawn. It would not surprise me to see *The Savannah Morning Times* come to the defense of Dr. Hammer. We could easily be portrayed as villains. The bottom line is that we have creditors who believe in our president. The local IRS office has held off on forcing us to pay all payroll taxes. If you take Dr. Hammer down, other things crucial to our operation will likely also fall.

Trustee Rayson. I will not be held hostage by the business community, or the threat of a host of other difficulties.

Chairman Eagles. Please wait to be recognized. Trustee Blakemon.

Trustee Blakemon. I agree with Trustee Winter. I think that Dr. Hammer has done grave harm to his relationship with this board; however, he still offers us a viable option for moving the college forward.

Chairman Eagles. Trustee Rayson.

Trustee Rayson. I call the previous question.

Chairman Eagles. The previous question has been called. All of those in favor please say Aye.

Aye!

Those who oppose the motion please say No.

Silence.

Chairman Eagles. All of those in favor of suspending the president with pay effective today please say Aye.

Aye. Only Trustee Rayson votes Aye.

Chairman Eagles. Those opposed please say No.

NO!

Chairman Eagles. The motion fails. Trustee Rayson.

Trustee Rayson. I move that the Board of Trustees of Stonewood College suspend the authority of Dr. Jason Hammer to manage the finances of the college. Under such a suspension he cannot obligate nor negotiate for the college contractually. If the suspension is approved, the executive committee, consisting of Chairman Eagles, and Trustees Rayson, Melvins and Raymondale will meet weekly with President Hammer and the appropriate vice presidents to review proposed spending and contracts and to approve or disapprove them as the committee deems proper.

Trustee Raymondale. I second the motion.

Chair Eagles. Is there discussion of the motion? Yes, Trustee Blakemon.

Trustee Blakemon. Such an action is bound to become known and I believe that it will hurt the college. Also I don't understand how it will help us with AACS. We may be shooting ourselves in the foot.

Chairman Eagles. Yes Trustee Stanmore.

Trustee Stanmore. Members of the board there is no evidence that the administration has mishandled any money. There is no evidence that in the daily operation of the college that we have had any fraud or theft. This administration has removed persons who prior to Dr. Hammer were stealing from the college – stealing while all of you sat on this board. This administration has operated in an exemplary manner. The motion is unwarranted by the facts and simply imposes a burden on the administration that compromises the effective management of Stonewood. The motion is actually unworthy of consideration.

Chairman Eagles. Trustee Raymondale.

Trustee Raymondale. There must be a consequence for the dishonesty of
Dr. Hammer. I favor the action and I also favor reconsidering the suspension at the April board meeting.

Chairman Eagles. Trustee Winter.

Trustee Winter. Members, I cannot support this action. It does not advance our agenda. It is not an action worthy of this board. You must consider the work done by Dr. Hammer - the tremendous accomplishments under difficult circumstances. This is an action, which could lead to President Hammer leaving Stonewood. No matter how you spin it, if Dr. Hammer leaves this board will receive and deserve great criticism. Additionally, his departure would weaken our efforts to be reaffirmed by AACS. I think that we seem to have a vendetta against this man, which is illogical. Mrs. Rayson you should withdraw your motion.

Chairman Eagles. Trustee Rayson.

Trustee Rayson. I shall not withdraw my motion. It is a motion that I believe protects our interests. I am not impressed by the argument that Dr. Hammer might leave. Let him leave! There are many talented and qualified persons in this community who could provide excellent leadership for this college. And the motion is not part of a vendetta.

Chairman Eagles. I am going to ask Dr. Melvins, provided there are no objections, to chair the meeting so that I can speak to this important issue. Dr. Melvins.

Dr. Melvins. Yes sir. The acting chair recognizes Trustee Eagles.

Trustee Eagles. I believe that it is important for the members of this board to be reminded that we are ultimately responsible for Stonewood College. I agree that there are many factors to consider in deciding on a course of action to deal with our current situation. However, we cannot allow those factors to cause us to shirk our responsibility. Now, I agree that Dr. Hammer has in some areas done a commendable job. This cannot mesmerize us and lead us to ignore that he deceived this board about the AACS meeting last December. Not all of our decisions will be easy; not all of them will be popular. We are not here to please others or any particular group. Let us resolve to proceed this evening with what best serves Stonewood College. I don't have to remind most of you that there was a time when people from the other community openly interfered with decisions made by this board. We are no longer so shackled and I expect you to stand for Stonewood.

Thank you Dr. Melvins.

Chairman Eagles. Trustee Winter.

Trustee Winter. Mr. Chairman I wish to offer a substitute motion. I move as a substitute that The Board of Trustees of Stonewood College place a letter of reprimand in the personnel file of Dr. Hammer admonishing him for dishonesty in the report that he made to the board in January 1986.

Trustee Blakemon. Second.

Chairman Eagles. It has been moved and seconded as a substitute motion that we place a letter of reprimand in the personnel file of Dr. Hammer admonishing him for dishonesty in the report that he made to the board in January 1986. Is there further discussion of these motions?

Chairman Eagles. Hearing none we shall proceed. The vote is on the substitute motion. Those in favor of the substitution please say Aye.

Aye is heard from Trustees Blakemon, Stanmore, and Winter.

Chairman Eagles. Those who oppose the substitution please say No.

No is heard from the other eight trustees.
Chairman Eagles. The substitute motion is rejected. Is there additional discussion of the original motion?

Chairman Eagles. Trustee Stanmore.

Trustee Stanmore. Mr. Chairman I move that we postpone indefinitely consideration of the motion to suspend the authority of the president.

Trustee Winter. Second.

Chairman Eagles. It has been moved and seconded that we postpone indefinitely consideration of the motion to suspend the authority of Dr. Hammer. Is there discussion? Trustee Stanmore.

Trustee Stanmore. I am convinced that we need more time to think about these matters. A delay will not keep us from returning at a later time to consideration of limiting the president's authority. A delay will keep from taking an action that damages all parties. We don't need to take an action that has been influenced by emotion. We need to be certain that we are not creating a larger problem for the college. Time is our ally.

Chairman Eagles. Is there additional discussion?

Silence.

Chairman Eagles. Those in favor of the motion to postpone indefinitely please say Aye.

Aye is heard from Trustees Blakemon, Stanmore, and Winter.

Chairman Eagles. Those who are opposed to the motion to postpone indefinitely please say No.

No is heard from the other eight trustees.

Chairman Eagles. The Noes have it and the motion to postpone indefinitely is rejected. Is there further discussion of the main motion?

Chairman Eagles. Hearing none we shall proceed. The vote is on the motion to suspend the authority of Dr. Jason Hammer to manage the finances of the college and that all decisions involving finances and contracts must be reviewed and approved or disapproved by the executive committee of the board. I believe that I captured it correctly.

Trustee Rayson. Yes sir, you did.

Chairman Eagles. Those in favor of the motion please say Aye.

Trustee Rayson. Mr. Chairman, if there are no objections, a roll call vote would be useful on this motion.

Chairman Eagles. Are there objections?

Chairman Eagles. Dr. Melvins, please take the vote by calling the roll.

Trustee Melvins. Trustee Avers – Aye.
Trustee Bellmede – Aye
Trustee Blakemon – No
Trustee Densley – Aye
Trustee Melvins – No
Trustee Pauls – Aye
Trustee Raymondale – No
Trustee Rayson – Aye
Trustee Stanmore – No
Trustee Velcome – Aye
Trustee Winter – No
Mr. Chairman, the Ayes have it, 6 to 5.

Chairman Eagles. The motion has passed. Therefore Dr. Hammer you will no longer exercise any authority over financial matters at Stonewood College effective immediately. This suspension in your authority will remain in effect until such time that the board decides to lift it. In two days you will receive a letter from the board describing the suspension. It will also give you the calendar of weekly meetings with the executive committee of the board. This concludes the agenda for this call meeting. You are reminded that our business is confidential. Thank you and good evening.

The lights dim on the boardroom as the board members exit. Dr. Hammer remains seated as the room goes dark.

After a minute the lights brighten on the kitchen of Trustee Rayson.

Narrator. The following Sunday morning.

Trustee Rayson calls Mrs. Bastrap from the phone in her kitchen. Mrs. Bastrap can be heard but not seen by the audience.

Trustee Rayson. Alexa, I wish you could have been there. The highly articulate Dr. Hammer was choked. Even now he does not know what hit him. We suspended his authority to make any financial decisions. I wonder if he told his best friend, LaPortier.

Mrs. Bastrap. I am glad that you limited him, but he is clever. So, be careful. He has that Stanmore guy helping him.

Trustee Rayson. I am going to continue to make his time at Stonewood as difficult as I can.

Mrs. Bastrap. If he leaves, do you think that they will give the position to you?

Trustee Rayson. I am going to have to work on Eagles, Raymondale, and Melvins.

Mrs. Bastrap. What about Reverend Winter?

Trustee Rayson. I don't think I could get his support. He really stood by Hammer and tried to persuade us to let him get away with lying to the board.

Mrs. Bastrap. Thanks Marva. This may be the beginning of getting our school back. Anyway I' ll talk to you later.

Trustee Rayson. Okay, bye.

The lights go dim on the kitchen of Trustee Rayson.

Unseen Mrs. Bastrap is heard by the audience calling the alumni association vice president, Mr. Walter Shreve. Mr. Shreve cannot be heard or seen.

Mrs. Bastrap. Hello Walter. Well it has happened – a fight between Hammer and the board.
Pause.
Mrs. Bastrap. That's right. They took away his authority to run the college.
Pause
Mrs. Bastrap. Yes, he's a figurehead. He can't spend or approve spending a single dime.
Pause
Mrs. Bastrap. Sure, that's exactly what it means. He must have been caught stealing money.
Pause
Mrs. Bastrap. You're right, it's a bombshell.
Pause
Mrs. Bastrap. We'll talk about association business later. I've got to go. Bye.

Silence.

Narrator. The next Monday morning Dr. Hammer meets with his cabinet.

The lights brighten on the boardroom.

Dr. Hammer. I must confidentially share with you that my authority to manage all financial matters at the college has been suspended by the board. I will meet with the executive committee of the board weekly in order to present to the committee pending transactions for review and approval/disapproval. At some of the meetings I will need Dr. Tullson. I shall make an effort to spare you the embarrassment of having to attend these meetings. The meeting at which this action was taken was very ugly. In accepting this position I did not understand the limitations of some of the board members. You should know that they found out about the disagreement that we had with AACS in Miami and used the fact that I had not been forthcoming in my report to essentially assassinate this administration. It won't take long before everyone in Savannah will know that we are no longer managing the college. Now, this could be a major problem for the board if AACS were informed of the board's interference in the administration of the college. I am not interested in creating any problems for them. With their leadership, the college will not survive.

Dr. Zillamen. The board members must not realize the destructive action that they have taken.

Dr. Hammer. I believe that a few of them do. I think the rest of them are so driven to hurt me that they are blinded to the consequences of their actions.

Dr. Tullson. We definitely don't need this kind of information to be known by the people with whom we do business. A few of them have actually started show us respect. The real problem for us is that the board is not confidential. This action by the board is bound to get out, and it probably already has. And you can be certain that there are distortions.

Dr. Lemon. Has our agenda changed?

Dr. Hammer. No, the agenda remains the same. We will give our best effort to ensure the future of the college. We will continue to strive for reaffirmation.

Dr. Zillamen. AACS is likely to make an inquiry.

Dr. Hammer. We will address it when it happens. Many problems may come our way over the next few months. We will address them as best we can and within the constraints the board has imposed.

Mr. Bessel. Dr. Hammer, how long do you plan to remain at the college?

Dr. Hammer. The board has made all of our positions tenuous. I could be terminated at any time. Although I have another year on my contract, I don't think that will deter the board members from terminating me.

Mr. Bessel. In other words, we would be wise to look for other options.

Dr. Hammer. Yes, although I found you here, you are now closely associated with me. I think the success we have had as a team has actually hurt you with some members of the board. I know that sounds strange, but logic and reason cannot be used to understand the situation we are in. We cannot afford to think that the excellent work we have done accrues any job security for us. I know that my tenure will not last beyond June 30, 1987 and that is extremely optimistic.

Dr. Zillamen. Do you expect that they will take other steps to make it more difficult to manage the college?

Dr. Hammer. Based on what I have seen, yes. But again, our approach must be to give our best effort as long as we are here.

The lights dim on the boardroom as Dr. Hammer continues the conversation with his cabinet.

Narrator. Spring has arrived. It is early April, approximately three weeks before the board meeting. The campus has been engulfed with rumors of mismanagement of the college's resources.

The lights brighten on the kitchen of Trustee Rayson. She has placed a call to Chairman Eagles. Chairman Eagles can be heard but not seen.

Trustee Rayson. Samuel, we must do something. Things are very bad at the college. I have been told repeatedly that Hammer and his people are stealing us blind. I knew that he was not to be trusted, but I had no idea that he would misuse his position.

Chairman Eagles. We have been monitoring closely all transactions since early March. There is no evidence of any theft.

Trustee Rayson. None that you have discovered. This man is clever and he has been wounded.

Chairman Eagles. Well, we have not found any theft. In fact it appears that they have done a fantastic job keeping everything operational.

Trustee Rayson. That may mean that the theft occurred before you started to look closely. Probably, those vice presidents who have become his personal lackeys are guilty of misusing our money. I heard that Dr. Zillamen is on travel three, maybe four times per month. We can't let Hammer's administration get away with abusing this college.

Chairman Eagles. Well let's see what other trustees think.

Trustee Rayson. Many of them suspect Hammer and his team of stealing from the college.

Chairman Eagles. Marva we'll do what's necessary to protect the college.

Trustee Rayson. Okay, I'll be in touch.

The lights dim on the kitchen of Trustee Rayson and then brighten as she makes another call.

Trustee Rayson. Hello, Alexa?
Mrs. Bastrap can be heard but not seen by the audience.

Mrs. Bastrap. Yes, Marva. How are you?

Trustee Rayson. Frustrated. I have heard over and over again that Hammer and his lackeys are stealing from the college. Something needs to be done to stop it.

Mrs. Bastrap. I have heard the rumors about the money and Hammer's girlfriend. You know the LaPortier thing has not gone away.

Trustee Rayson. You are close to Reverend Raymondale. Give him a call and let him know what you have heard about money being stolen and the need for the board to protect the college. Ask him if the chairman is aware.

Mrs. Bastrap. I'll do it right away.

Trustee Rayson. And call Pauls and Densley. They don't like Hammer and often vote to keep him in check.

Mrs. Bastrap. Okay, bye.

As Trustee Rayson hangs up the lights again dim on her kitchen.

Narrator. It is now the latter part of April. The annual meeting of the Stonewood College Board of Trustees has been called to order by Chairman Eagles. Trustee Melvins has completed the roll call.

The lights brighten on the boardroom.

Chairman Eagles. We are going to modify the agenda, which consists of reports from our standing committees. Without objection we are going to insert at the top of the agenda financial mismanagement.

Silence.

Chairman Eagles. Since our last call meeting I have received in writing and by telephone allegations that this administration has stolen money from the college. The volume is unprecedented. I was determined to ignore these allegations; however, given that some of the sources are highly credible I am obligated to inform you that we must take steps to make certain that the college has not been plundered. President Hammer.

Dr. Hammer. Last year the audit was clean. The federal audit was clean, which is unprecedented for the college. Audits for this year will be clean. We are currently monitored by the executive committee of the board. We have been frugal in spending money and our purchases are tied to programs for our students. We have paid vendors promptly and we have gained the confidence of local businesses. To allege that money has been stolen is an affront to me and my administrative team, personally and professionally. You should be ashamed to smear the hard work and sacrifices made by this administration by such an allegation. I have also heard the rumors of mismanagement. I understand. You the members of this board are the source of these vile allegations. What you have heard are the echoes, the reverberations of the poisonous language you have put out about me and the members of my administrative team. In spite of what we have endured, we have always given our best effort to each task, to each assignment.

Chairman Eagles. Thank you Dr. Hammer. Now let me tell you what is going to happen. Each member of your team including you will be audited by a firm chosen by the board. Travel, spending, hiring, terminations, all events with a financial consequence will be audited. You and the vice presidents are instructed to cooperate with the auditors and to make all records available to them. As a result of the individual audits, we shall seek recovery of any and all funds owed to the college. Is that clear?

Dr. Hammer. Yes Mr. Chairman.

Chairman Eagles. You will be notified in writing of the audit firm selected and the start date for these audits. Now let's move forward with the agenda.

The lights dim on the boardroom as the meeting continues. The lights again brighten on the boardroom.

Chairman Eagles. Well that concludes the agenda. Yes, Dr. Hammer is there something else?

Dr. Hammer. Yes, Mr. Chairman. I wish to announce that I have decided to submit my resignation as President of Stonewood College effective July 31, 1986. I shall work to make certain that the next president has reports that will provide an assessment and status of all divisions and major offices in the college.

Chairman Eagles. Thank you Dr. Hammer. If there are no objections, we will stand adjourned.

The lights dim on the boardroom as the members exit.

Narrator. The next Monday President Hammer meets with his cabinet.

The lights brighten on the boardroom.

Dr. Hammer. As you now know, I informed the board last week that I shall leave the college on July 31, 1986. What I did not inform the board of is the fact that I shall become on August 15 the President of the Eastern Georgia Community College System. This shall become publically known this Sunday in an article on my departure in *The Savannah Morning Times*. The article will praise our accomplishments and raise questions about the leadership of the board.

Dr. Zillamen. Congratulations on the new position. I can imagine that the chairman and members of the executive committee are busy trying to figure out who could be convinced to replace you.

Dr. Hammer. Yes and I shall play no role. Please work to maintain your respective areas. I cannot speak to the subject of how much time you have. I expect the subject will come up in my next conversation with the chairman. Additionally, the board has decided to audit our individual actions, transactions and decisions that involved money. An audit firm will be selected by the board and conduct the audit within the next few weeks. Cooperate and go about your work in the usual way.

Dr. Lemon. Will there be an opportunity for any of us at EGCC?

Dr. Hammer. At this point in time no. If that changes, I will let you know.

Mr. Bessel. I am glad that you beat them to the punch. I hope the article on Sunday reveals to the public the real problems at this college.

Dr. Hammer. I don't expect that the article will go that far. After all, who would believe the pathologies?

Dr. Tullson. You know they will attempt to reverse many of the actions we took.

Dr. Hammer. That will be difficult for the major projects, but I expect the policy changes we made to be easy targets. Dr. Zillamen, please call a meeting of the faculty and staff so that I can inform the community of my resignation. Now lets focus on the fall semester.

The lights dim on the boardroom as Dr. Hammer continues to lead the discussion.

Narrator. It is early June and Dr. Hammer is in the weekly cabinet meeting.

The lights brighten on the boardroom.

Dr. Hammer. I have the results from the individual audits. There were no findings of mismanagement of college funds. In fact, because we have not been reimbursed for many of our travel expenses the college owes money to each one of us. The total amounts to about $12,600. I had a conversation with the chairman about the audits. I pointed out to him that an organization chosen by him, that sent a team of people who went through our files, pulled receipts for confirmation, and interviewed scores of people found what I had told him and the board members. We have not mismanaged any money. It was clear to me that he was extremely disappointed that he did not get from the audits the smoking gun that he so badly wanted. I asked him if he would make certain that we received the reimbursements that his audit firm established as legitimate. He would not respond. He said that the board must study the reports. The chairman did inform me that the executive committee wants all the vice presidents to resign and leave prior to my exit. You may give me your letters at your convenience. You should inform your respective divisions around the date that you give me your letter. I will write letters of recommendation and assist each of you in obtaining employment.

Dr. Zillamen. Mr. Eagles and some of the board members are truly mean-spirited. They need us and yet they are willing to hurt the institution in order to hurt us. Whatever they do wrong over the next year, they will blame us. You can be certain that being here during the last two years will likely follow us for a long time. I hope that they don't destroy it this coming semester. That they will destroy it is without doubt. And sadly we can't help them. Although I have tenure, I shall take this opportunity to leave.

Dr. Tullson. You can be certain that the chairman will attempt to get someone who in his thinking eclipses Dr. Hammer. It won't matter that the person may be ill suited for the work. And what will never be understood is how we were able to accomplish so much. In fact, our accomplishments will evaporate in the wake of board interference and a complete misunderstanding of the forces that can destroy the college.

Dr. Lemon. My staff and the student leaders are going to be devastated by my departure. I don't know how I can explain to them that my commitment and my desire to achieve did not change. This will not play well. It will seem that we all just ran away because the work was difficult.

Dr. Hammer. You will find the appropriate words. You cannot say that the chairman and the executive committee forced you to resign. This is what Chairman Eagles wants. I urge you not to engage in a fight with the board. Just move on. Some individuals will accuse you of causing the downfall of this college. Deny it and move on. Any thoughtful person who cares to understand what happened here will be able to do it.

Dr Zillamen. I don't think that's true. Some of it will be easy. It will be difficult to understand the paternalistic and racist role of the league, the level of ignorance, backwardness, and jealousy of some members of the board and the alumni association, the dishonest role of AACS and the confluence of years of bad administrative decisions. What will be easy will be for the board, the alumni association, and even AACS to blame the problem at Stonewood on this administration.

Dr. Hammer. You are probably correct. Let's discuss summer commencement.

The lights dim on the boardroom.

Narrator. In early July the vice presidents submit letters of resignation. In late July the president calls one last meeting of the cabinet.

The lights brighten on the boardroom.

Dr. Hammer. Well in a few weeks we will all be gone. I thought that we should meet for one last update. As you know I shall take over as President of EGCC around August 15. Can we share what we will be doing in the near future?

Dr. Zillamen. I have accepted a faculty position at the University of Atlanta.

Dr. Tullson. I have accepted the position of vice president for business affairs at the University of Charlotte.

Dr. Lemon. I have accepted a faculty position Melrose State University.

Mr. Bessel. I have accepted the position of controller over at the University of Augusta.

Dr. Hammer. So Nathan two of us will remain in the neighborhood. I spoke with Chairman Eagles a few days ago. He informed me that the board has selected Dr. Broadus Nullfield, President Emeritus of Allenville State University in Alabama.

Dr. Zillamen. Dr. Nullfield has never worked at a private college and he has no record of raising money. He is not used to the kind of sacrifices we have made to keep this college afloat. It seems to me to be a strange choice.

Dr. Hammer. I am told that Dr. Nullfield and the chairman are good friends. As you may have suspected Mrs. Rayson attempted to persuade the chairman and other board members that she should be the next president of the college. She was shocked that even the alumni association and Mrs. Bastrap said that she was ill suited for such a position.

Dr. Tullson. Do you think that Dr. Nullfield understands the financial picture of the college?

Dr. Hammer. I doubt it. I can't believe that a man in his position would accept an assignment with such a high probability of failure. Any understanding of who we are and what we did, and attempted to do would persuade many administrators not to come. Since I announced my resignation, the projected fall enrollment has declined. If I were Dr. Nullfield I would be concerned with how I am going to meet the September payroll. Such a prospect will probably come as a shock to him. He will soon realize that he has been misled. And it is unlikely that the board will unite behind him. Although I told the chairman that we would help if called upon, I doubt that we shall ever be called.

Dr. Zillamen. What about Jackson Stanmore?

Dr. Hammer. I believe that he plans to resign his position on the board later this fall.

Dr. Zillamen. Does that mean that the league no longer has any interest in the college?

Dr. Hammer. I leave that for you to decide.

The lights dim on the boardroom as the cabinet members exchange handshakes and hugs. Dean Bennings emerges from the wall.

Dean Bennings. Another phase in the history of Stonewood has ended, one that leaves it a far weaker institution. Dr. Nullfield is a good person, but he has no idea about what he now faces. Chairman Eagles will go to great lengths to see him succeed. The board will become dissatisfied with his leadership as the members slowly realize the opportunity they lost by not supporting Dr. Hammer. Trustee Rayson will try to prove that she should be president by being critical of Dr. Nullfield. Trustee Raymondale will look for ways to distance himself from the board. His questioning of the need for the college will become more common. Trustees Winter and Blakemon will grow frustrated with the pettiness of some board members. Dr. Nullfield will appoint vice presidents from the faculty and staff. They are good people but they lack the talent and abilities of the departing vice presidents. I regret that we did not do more to prepare our successors to function in a more demanding and competitive environment.

Narrator. One year later. (July 1987)

Dean Bennings emerges from the boardroom wall.

Dean Bennings. The college is still on probation. The board has a new chairman, Reverend Albert Densley. Using the credit that the former administration had established the college now owes local vendors slightly more than one million dollars.

Enrollment in the spring semester dropped to 1,000 students when it was announced that the college had again failed to have its accreditation reaffirmed. Reverend Densley and some board members including Trustee Rayson want Stonewood College to file bankruptcy. Interestingly, the college still has a football team. Payroll problems have mounted. The faculty is owed three months salary from last academic year. The current faculty is about a fourth of what it was three years ago. The decline in all areas has been rapid and steep. Many alumni members openly blame the Hammer administration for destroying the college.

Narrator. Eighteen months later. (January 1989)

Dean Bennings emerges from the boardroom wall.

Dean Bennings. Well it happened about a year ago in Miami. AACS withdrew the accreditation of the college. Enrollment in the spring semester was 200 students, most of whom were seniors. This past summer the board filed for bankruptcy. Dr Nullfield resigned effective last June 30th. He cited declining health as the reason. In early July the board met and decided to close the college. Many people thought that the bankruptcy judge would sell the land, buildings, furniture, equipment, books, pictures, and other materials in order to pay the IRS, vendors, faculty and staff, and the retirement fund. The judge accepted bids and announced the other day the sale of the campus as is for the sum of one million dollars to businesswoman Marva Rayson. The sale price was shockingly low to most observers and was not enough to pay off the IRS. It meant that faculty and staff members would never recover the money owed them. How could the judge reason that one million dollars was sufficient to close the Stonewood case? How could a former trustee offer an amount that was not sufficient to purchase a single building on the campus? Was she not ashamed to have acquired the college for an amount of money that ensured the suffering of former faculty, staff and students? Was there some other score to settle at the expense of the college, and its loyal faculty and staff? Did the alumni rise up in protest? No. Did anyone criticize the painful way that Stonewood was dragged to the grave? No. Sadly, no tributes, no eulogies were offered.

The lights on Dean Bennings dim and go dark.

A minute goes by and the lights again brighten on Dean Bennings.

Requiem

Pomp and Circumstance is played softly.

Dean Bennings. It is done. My school, once magnificent in its quest, once glorious in its service, is gone. Some know its story, some understand its journey, and some regret its tragic loss. I leave you with words that I find fitting.

In the end your closing bore no resemblance
To the nobility of your service.
It was not registered as a special day on any calendar
No proclamations of recognition were issued.
So persuasive had been the forces against you
That supporters wept not openly
But far from the view of others.

The years since your departure
Find your mission not taken by others.
The claims made against you
The analysis used to chart your closing
Yielded no institution to take your mantel
And it did greatly weaken education in America.
Is there justice for you?

Who has seen the faces
Of those you might have saved?
Who feels the absence
And the pain that pierces so deep our society?
What ill framed arguments
Could mesmerize us to accept the irrational closing
Of an institution with great work yet to be done?

Though we failed to preserve
What had been given to us
Though we failed to pass on to other generations
An institution that might have saved them as it did us
Though we are poorer and wrought with regret
We often recall your majestic service
And we are inspired to preserve other institutions.[2]

Pomp and Circumstance continues to play softly as the curtain slowly falls.
